Trident

Mayham Makers

Satan's Cowboys MC
Book 1

Khloe Wren

Dedication

To all the fiery redhead women who have never quite found their place in this world: Jacie is for you.

Bonus dedication: to the original Red Queen, Dorothy F. Shaw.
Without her support, this book may never have gotten finished!

Glossary

I've written this book in US English as it's set in Texas and Hawaii, however, Jacie is Australian so there are Aussie words in her scenes with Aussie spellings. And Trident is Hawaiian, so there are some Hawaiian words in his scenes. Especially later, once they're in Hawaii. I've included a glossary to help you out with these words.

Australian:
Arse: Ass
C'mon: 'come on', hurry up, get moving
Lemon, Lime Bitters: A popular non alcoholic mixed drink made with clear lemonade, lime cordial, and bitters.
Loo: Toilet/bathroom
Vegemite: A very salty, thick, dark brown spread made from leftover brewers' yeast extract with various vegetable and spice additives.

Hawaiian:
Aloha: Hello
Braddah/s, Brah/s: Brother/s

Fucka: Fucker

Greet with breath: a special greeting shared being two Hawaiian people

Hale: Home

Hawai'i: Hawaii

Kaua'i: Kauai, Hawaiian Island

Keiki: Child

Lū'au: party/celebration

Makua: Dad

Makuahine: Mother

Makua kāne: Father

Māmā: Mom

O'ahu: Hawaiian Island

Pàhoa: a wooden bladed weapon with shark teeth down the curved edge

Throw Cracks: throw a punch, take someone down/out

Ula'ula Mõ'ī: My red queen

Japanese:

Mekake: Concubine/mistress

Texan/Biker:

Colors/Cut: Vest worn by MC brothers and their Old Ladies

Mustang: a wild horse

Old lady: Biker's wife/partner

Well quality: cheapest, lowest quality alcohol available

Chapter 1

Jacie

Saturday, July 4th, 2020

My face burned hot with embarrassment and frustration as the cute guy I'd been flirting with took off like his arse was on fire after my big brother, Taz, had growled something to him. Most likely a threat that involved bodily harm.

"I cannot believe I moved halfway around the world to be closer to him. How could he do this to me? And at my birthday party!"

Flick, my heavily pregnant sister-in-law, winced as she shrugged a shoulder, then wrapped the arm not cradling her baby bump around my waist and guided me across the Charon MC clubhouse yard toward her friends. The ladies were standing only a short distance from the rear entrance to the building, no doubt because most of them were like Flick, heavily pregnant, and didn't want to be too far from the bathroom.

"For starters, as you're well aware, this ain't your birthday party, sis. It's a Charon and Satan's Cowboys joint club Independence Day barbecue. Sadly, now that you live here in the States, you gotta share your birthday with Fourth of July celebrations."

I also, apparently, got to spend my birthday surrounded by pregnant women to rub in the fact that, for me, finding a bloke to settle down and have some kids of my own with seemed an impossibility. And if Taz kept scaring away any guy I even tried to talk to, I didn't see that changing anytime soon.

Trying to focus on something positive, I glanced toward the setting sun that was painting the sky a beautiful array of colors.

"At least it's warm. July is winter in Australia, and it's pretty much always rained on my birthday."

Flick laughed. "Chances of us getting rain here in Texas, in July, is pretty damn slim, so no worries there. But seriously, Jacie, Taz is always going to see you as his precious baby sister. And he's always going to want to protect you, especially at a party this big with so many single men here looking to celebrate."

She didn't need to voice what the biggest reason he was so up in my business was: that he'd believed I'd been dead for the past twenty-three years. While I totally understood why he'd be extra protective after learning I was alive and well, it didn't make his antics any less annoying.

"But I'm a grown arse adult! And I've been living here for over eight months now. He needs to get over it already. How the fuck am I ever going to have a life if he keeps this shit up?"

As I wondered if maybe I'd have to move away from Bridgewater and just come for visits, tears burned the backs of my eyes, but I forced them away, along with that thought.

Silk, who was the old lady of one of Taz's best mates, Eagle, rubbed her hand over her large belly as she snorted out a short laugh. "Oh, honey, I hear you. Try growing up here with your uncle as the VP. You gotta get real sneaky if you want a sex life. On the upside, when a guy does stick around, you know he's for real because no man is gonna put up with this many overbearing, overprotective brothers if they're not damn serious about you. Welcome to being a Daughter of the Club, doll."

When she gazed over toward her man, her expression softening and going all gooey, I turned away with a huff. It wasn't fair that I had to be surrounded by all these loved up women when I wasn't allowed even a chance to find the same for myself. Zara, Mac's old lady, who was, naturally, also pregnant, handed me a bottle of beer with a sympathetic smile.

"Only reason you got as far as you did with that prospect was because he's a newbie. And you're not wearing a cut."

I screwed up my nose after I took a long swig of the cold brew.

"And that's why I'm refusing to have a vest. Cut. Whatever you want to call it. I am not a Daughter of the Club, and I'm definitely not going to allow my brother, or any other man for that matter, to brand me as his property. No way, no how."

I couldn't understand why so many of the wives in the club happily let their men 'patch' them. Nope. That was not going to be my life. I was an all modern, independent woman. I even rode my own bike. No riding bitch behind some bloke for me.

Zara chuckled. "Babe, you're a Daughter of the Club. You don't need to be wearing the patch for that to be true. And honestly? Taz would probably be on your case a lot less if you agreed to wear one. Being property of a brother in a club is about protection, not ownership.

It's him declaring to the world that you're loved and cared for."

Rolling my eyes, I took another long drink. Beer was not going to be strong enough to get me through this evening. "Nope, I'm pretty sure it's the ownership thing. And Taz wouldn't need to be all over me like white on rice. Every man involved in the club would see that little patch with the heart wrapped in barbed wire on it, turn tail and run. Any bloke not in the club would see the Charon MC patch on the back and do the same bloody thing."

After draining the last of my beer, I broke away from the women, tossing my now empty bottle into a trash can. "I'm heading in to get something stronger. Back in a bit."

Maybe, I added silently to myself. With the weather being so nice, and the fact there were plenty of drinks and food out in the yard, I doubted anyone would be inside. I could just claim a booth in the main room and drink myself stupid all by my lonesome in a dark corner.

Before any of them could stop me, I headed inside, wishing my girls Nevaeh, Mirabelle and Sparrow were here. The old ladies were great and all, but they were in a different phase of their lives than I was, popping out babies and settling down. Since it was becoming obvious I wouldn't be joining them any time soon, I figured I'd focus on simply having some fun and messing around. And I was pretty sure Nevaeh, Mirabelle and Sparrow felt the same way. Well, after all the abuse and torture Mirabelle had been through, she was all about having fun that didn't involve men at all, which was fine with us. We'd always take care of her. But sadly, my trio of besties were all on childcare duties tonight. If it hadn't been my birthday, I'd have joined them in looking after all the babies and kids of the club and earning some cash. Instead, I was here celebrating my twenty-sixth birthday without my girl crew.

Making my way down the hallway, I shook those thoughts away. Next weekend would be my real birthday celebration. There was a massive book signing happening up in Dallas: "MMM: Motorcycles, Mobsters & Mayhem." The four of us were heading up there for a girls' weekend. It was going to be epic, and I was crazy excited to meet several of my favorite authors, along with, hopefully, some of their hunky cover models. Pretend bikers and mobsters were so much safer to drool over than real ones. Especially since Taz would be back here in Bridgewater fussing over his pregnant wife and far away from me in Dallas.

Sliding onto a stool at the bar, I ran my gaze over the prospect that stood behind it. Not too shabby at all, but his wide-eyed expression told me all I needed to know. Unlike the last one, this prospect knew who I was.

"Hey, Jacie, uh, what can I get for you? You know there's beer and wine and shit out the back, yeah?"

Rolling my eyes on a sigh, I shook my head. "Just make me an Old Fashioned, and I'll go sit over on the other side of the room, far away from you so you don't need to fear Taz coming after you."

He rubbed a palm over the back of his neck. "Uh, well, you know most of the brothers just want straight up liquor. I got no clue how to make any fancy shit."

"Fuck my life," I muttered under my breath. It's not like an Old Fashioned was a fancy bloody cocktail or something. He wouldn't have even needed to use a damn shaker to make it.

"Move to the side and I'll show you."

He bolted out from behind the bar so fast, if I'd blinked at the wrong time, I wouldn't have seen him move.

"Nah, it's fine. I'll learn some other time. I, uh, need a bathroom break anyhow. You just do your thing, and I'll come back after you're done."

Shaking my head at the fleeing coward, I moved behind the bar and started to grab what I needed. Luckily, I'd suspected this was how my night would go and had brought in some of my special simple syrup earlier for just this purpose. It wasn't the first time I'd added to the clubhouse's bar. Within weeks of moving to Bridgewater, I'd added a bottle of Bitters because I loved a good *Lemon, Lime Bitters*, but it seemed like Americans hadn't discovered that one yet.

Scanning the bottles, I chuckled and reached for the *Still Austin* bottle of Straight Rye Whiskey. The label had a long-eared rabbit on it, and it also had a silver sticker claiming it had won some award, so it should work just fine for my drink. I was just placing the bottle down when a deep, gravelly voice had me pausing.

"Whatcha making, girlie?"

With a frown, I glared toward the voice and lost my breath for a few seconds. Holy smokes. An older man, maybe in his mid-forties sat at a stool and was leaning against the other side of the bar. His steel-gray hair was buzz cut on the sides and the top was in neat cornrows. I had no idea how long it would be when it was down but, for some strange reason, I wanted to know.

Like a lot of the guys, he wore his leather cut with no shirt underneath and damn, the man took care of himself. Old-school black inkwork covered muscular biceps that twitched under my gaze. His pecs were solid pads of muscle, which were also covered in tattoos and although the bar hid his abs, I bet they were as defined as the rest of his torso. My gaze caught on the chunky chains around his neck, trying to read what was written below a skull on a large pendant that hung from one of them.

His low chuckle had my cheeks heating, as my gaze jumped up to his face to see one eyebrow raised, laughter in his dark irises and a sexy smirk on his lips. He lifted a palm to stroke his beard as he spoke.

"See something you like, girlie?"

Oh, yeah, that's right. I was gonna yell at him for calling me a girl. Whoever the hell he was.

I pointed a finger at his chest. "I am not a child."

His dark gaze lowered, and instinctively I put my shoulders back and stood taller as he took his turn to take in his fill of me. Flames curled deep within me as his eyes paused on my breasts on his trip back up my body. They were small, only a B cup, but they were perky and the pushup bra I currently wore had them looking more like DDs. *I hoped.* It was what the tag on it had claimed it would do, anyhow.

"You are most certainly all woman, Jacie Lewis."

That had me frowning again. "I don't believe we've ever met. How the bloody hell do you know who I am?"

Standing, he half turned to flash the back of his cut to reveal the head of a grinning red devil wearing a cowboy hat along with the words "Satan's Cowboys MC" and "Cutler".

"I ain't a Charon, baby. That's why we've not met. Name's Trident. I'm an enforcer for the Satan's Cowboys MC. And I know who you are, 'cause we all do. Taz's long lost baby sis, thought dead, come back to life. Gossip spreads real fast in MCs, especially shit like that."

My face heated again. Dammit. I didn't want to be infamous for something that wasn't even my doing. It wasn't like the authorities had given me a say in what they did when I'd been a kid.

"Well, while I might be a lot younger than my brother, I am not a child. Haven't been for a damn long time. So don't call me girlie."

He raised that brow at me again, which he needed to stop doing. When he did, his eyes glinted in this way that had me squeezing my thighs together.

"How old are you exactly? Should you even be behind that bar? We get raided by the cops, Scout gonna be in trouble for underage drinking?"

His voice was laced with humor, but it still pissed me off. I grabbed a bottle of beer from the fridge and slammed it down on the bar in front of him. Hopefully, when he opened it, it'd spray all over him.

"Take your drink and fuck off. There's more outside if you want a refill. I do not need your shit tonight."

He chuckled, the sound deep with a little gravel to it, like his voice. Damn. Why did he have to be an asshole? Because between that voice and all his inked-up muscles, I wouldn't have minded taking him for a ride to celebrate my birthday. But not with that attitude of his. Nope. My next man was gonna be a nice guy.

I ignored my inner voice laughing at me. Just because I'd never dated a nice guy in my life, or even been remotely attracted to one, didn't mean I couldn't change. Right?

"You got gumption. Like that. Not too many men who'd do what you've done, let alone a woman. Especially here, with how the Charons fall under SCMC rule. Most folks in this place would trip over themselves to keep any of us happy, but not you. Interesting. Dangerous, but interesting. And I don't want a beer. As you pointed out, I could have gotten one outside."

I rolled my eyes and got back to mixing my drink. If he wasn't going to go the hell away, I'd just ignore him.

Well, try to. Damn man took up a whole lot of space despite the fact he wasn't overly tall. He was probably the same height as Taz, around six-two, but he had this presence about him. One that demanded people take him seriously. Stupid MCs and all their rules. But I hadn't been raised to be a wallflower. If someone pissed me off, they were gonna know about it. I didn't care who they were, or where they were from.

Chapter 2

Trident

Jacie was turning out to be quite an intriguing puzzle. She definitely wasn't who I'd expected her to be from what I'd heard about her. Her *take no shit* attitude certainly didn't match her sweet looks, that was for sure.

As I looked my fill, I took the beer bottle and began to pick at the label. I sure as shit wasn't going to open the damn thing with how she'd slammed it down. I wasn't looking for a beer shower.

She was a pretty little thing. Short; I'd guess five-one, maybe five-two. Long, wavy, naturally light red hair, pale skin with some freckles. She looked like a fucking teenager. All sweet and pure. But that mouth on her soon proved that idea wrong. She was no innocent angel. Although, considering she was both Australian and Taz's sister, I really should have expected at least a little sass.

And fuck me, because if she'd been that sweet little girlie I'd first thought she was, I could have done what I'd originally intended to, then walked away. But not now. That steel spine of hers tripped my switch in a big way, and I wanted more. My rock-hard cock throbbed in agreement.

When she set an unlabeled bottle of dark liquid down next to the other shit she'd gathered, I frowned at it.

"What the fuck is that?"

Since she hadn't told me what she was making when I'd asked earlier, I had no clue. It wasn't like I was a connoisseur of mixed drinks or some shit. Since I mostly just did shots with the brothers, I barely tasted any alcohol I drank. Most of the crap we had at the SCMC clubhouse was well quality and wasn't worth fucking tasting anyhow.

She glared at me again. Fuck, that fire that flared in her blue irises did something for me too. The throbbing in my groin was getting uncomfortable, and if I didn't think she'd throw a bottle at my head for it, I'd adjust myself, but self-preservation had me putting up with my dick hurting. For the moment, at least.

"Why are you still here bothering me?"

I gave her a sly grin, more than ready for our next round of banter. "Where the fuck did you think I'd be exactly? Especially since I'm still waitin' on some answers."

She tilted her head back, closing her eyes for a second before looking at me again with a huff. The movement pushed her tits up and drew my attention their way. As I thought about what color her nipples might be, what they'd taste like as I ran my tongue over each one, nipping them when they tightened up...

"Oh, for fucks sake. My face is up here. You want answers?" She lifted the unlabeled bottle. "This is simple syrup. Yes, it's not clear like normal. That's because I make it special. The way I like it. The wvay my dad taught me. And I'm making myself an Old Fashioned. Now you can go the hell away."

Yeah, that sass of hers did something for me in a big way.

"Think I'll stay right where I am and try one of those drinks you're making myself. Why dontcha grab another glass and make me one too?"

When she clenched her fists against the bar top as she looked down at her feet, I barely resisted the urge to chuckle. A true redhead, her temper flared fast and bright. Making the most of her looking away, I adjusted my dick so it wasn't pressed up against my zipper. My thin boxer-briefs hadn't formed much of a barrier. Thankfully, she didn't look back at me until after I got done. I could only imagine what fury she'd have spit my way if she'd busted me.

"What do I need to do or say to make you go the fuck away and leave me alone?"

"Why you want me gone?" I cocked my head toward the rear of the clubhouse. "From what I heard out there, you're looking for some male attention tonight. And let me tell you, babe, I ain't some pissant prospect. I'm not scared of your brother, or any other Charon, for that matter. So why you trying so hard to send me on my way?"

She froze for a few moments, just blinking. Guess she either hadn't thought it through, or didn't like I'd caught the earlier altercation in the yard. Sucked to be her, because everyone out there had caught that drama. Taz hadn't exactly been subtle about ripping that prospect a new asshole for daring to touch his precious baby sis. I'd also heard how Animal and a few of the other SCMC brothers had proceeded to turn getting into her panties into a fucking game. They wanted to mess her up as much as possible, all in the name of getting even with Taz and his old lady, Flick, for what she'd pulled at our clubhouse a couple of years back.

That was something I wasn't ever gonna stand by and watch happen to any woman. So, pretending like I hadn't heard their bullshit, I casually strode off and followed her when she'd come in here. While I was with her, she'd be safe from my club brothers and their games. Since I'd spotted three of them come and go from the room so far and expected to see more, I knew I'd cop some shit later for cock-blocking them. But such was life. And a small price to pay to keep the little spitfire in front of me safe.

Although, when I'd followed her, I hadn't expected to like the girl, uh, woman. Made me feel better that despite all her hissing and spitting, the fact that she hadn't called her brother in, told me she wasn't really all that upset with me hanging around. And I hadn't missed her checking me out earlier. She liked what she saw and was feeling me. No matter what she tried to tell me or herself.

Wanting to break the silence, I nodded to the dark simple syrup. "Didn't think you liked your dad. Why copy his favorite drink?"

Her head jerked up as she leveled a glare with so much heat in it, if I'd been a lesser man, I might have run away. Gotta love a fiery redhead.

"I *hated* my sperm donor. He murdered my mum and tried to kill me. Then came after my brother and his family to do the same bloody thing to them. I was proud to be able to help take that bastard out. I have never wanted a damn thing from that piece of shit."

Straightening on the stool, I held up my palms. "Just a question, babe. You were the one who mentioned him."

With a shake of her head, the fire left her gaze as she grabbed another glass, setting it beside hers before she started pouring various liquids into them.

"I meant my adoptive dad. The man who raised me."

"But he didn't take in Taz? I don't get that. None of the stories I've heard about either of you has answered that one."

Finished with the various bottles, she put them away before moving to add a scoop of ice into each glass. She grabbed for a jar of maraschino cherries and popped one into each drink before she set one in front of me gently.

"Your drink." She didn't remove her hand from the glass, even when I took advantage and slid my fingers over hers, loving how my calluses caught on her smooth skin, while I looked her in the eye when she started speaking again. "And I don't know you nearly well enough to be giving you any of my family history. Especially since I'm pretty sure it'll just end up being added to the club gossip mill."

Having said what she clearly thought would be her final words to me, she pulled her hand away before focusing on doing a quick tidy up, wiping down the bar top, before she grabbed her glass and moved out from behind the bar. Turning, I watched the sway of her hips until she slipped into one of the booths along the rear wall. She'd picked one deep in the shadows, clearly wanting to be alone. Shouldn't have been a big ask since we were the only ones in here. The coward of a prospect who'd been manning the bar hadn't returned, and with the weather being so nice, along with the fact there was food and drink outside, no one was hanging out in here.

That didn't mean I slacked off in keeping an eye on the whole room, all entrances and exits. It'd been a long damn time since I hadn't kept track of everything going on around me at all times. I'd learned that lesson the hard way a long damn time ago. It wasn't one I'd ever forget.

When Animal came barreling down the hallway, I cursed. Looked like Jacie had gotten all the alone time she was going to get. It was either me or Animal, and he hadn't gotten his road name because he rescued critters in his spare time. Taking a sip of my drink as I rose from the stool, I shook my head and took a bigger mouthful. Damn, this shit was good. Maybe I'd been missing opportunities to actually enjoy drinking all these years by just doing shots of cheap crap. They hadn't taken her long to make, so it couldn't be that hard for me to learn how, right? Might be nice to finish off a day with one of these out on my porch.

Be even better if she were there with me, making them for us both.

"Fucker." I muttered under my breath in response to that invasive thought that had come out of nowhere. Like I suddenly had some sort of white picket fence fantasy for my future that I'd never wanted before.

I'd only made it a few steps toward her when Animal caught up to me, gripping my shoulder with his large palm to stop my progress. "Hey, Trident."

While I'd monitored his approach, I hadn't attempted to move out of his way. There was no avoiding this conversation, and I'd prefer have it over this side of the room, rather than in front of Jacie at her booth.

"What you doin' with my little sweet butt? You pissed you got left outta our bet, old man?"

I took another mouthful of my drink before I responded. Letting the mellow flavor help level me out so I could resist the urge I had to knock my club brother out.

"She ain't your anything, Animal. And she ain't a

sweet butt. You know full well I won't allow you to chew up and spit out a Charon Daughter of the Club. Viper will have you by the balls if you do. We need this club and access to their bunker."

I would have stepped in to save any woman from him when he was jazzed up like he currently was, but he wouldn't understand that. The fact that our club needed the Charons on our side so we could use an old bunker on their land to help run shit through was something he should understand. Animal scanned the room until he spotted Jacie in her hiding spot, then he grinned like the fucking lunatic he could be. I turned to see her frowning our way.

"First up, she ain't wearing no patch, so she ain't shit to the club, and second, they'd never know it was me."

I shrugged his hand off my shoulder, getting his attention focused back on me.

"You're lying to me and yourself if you believe that shit for a second. She's a brother's sister. That makes her club property, regardless of what she is or isn't wearing. You're thinking with your ego, wanting to get even with Flick and her old man, Taz. To do that, they'd need to know it was you who fucked up his sister. You go through with this, and it'll spiral outta control in a fucking heartbeat. You wanna be the one to explain to Viper why we can't run our gear through their bunker anymore?"

He bared his teeth my way, an unnatural fire in his gaze that confirmed what I'd already suspected. He'd taken something and was tripping hard. "You just want her tight little pussy all to yourself. Selfish prick. Wait until I tell the others. Don't want me to chew her up and spit her out? Fine. I'll come at you instead."

Fuck my life. It wasn't that I didn't believe and

follow the club's rule of Brothers First, Brothers Forever, but Animal was way outta line here. The fact he was flying high on something didn't help. Fucking drugs, man. I'd never touch them. They stole your control. I was doing more than just protecting Jacie. We'd been losing shipments left and right before we'd started using the hidden bunker here in Bridgewater to break up the runs. I blew out a breath and shook my head, not taking my gaze off my club brother.

"You might have the brute strength, Animal. But we both know I got more skill and can take you. You want me to hand your ass to you again? Tell me the time and place, and I'll happily vent some frustration by knocking you down a couple pegs. But it ain't gonna be in the middle of the Charon's clubhouse, yeah?"

With a growl and his body vibrating with a rage I knew I'd have to deal with sooner rather than later, he spun on his booted heel and stormed back down the hallway. Watching him go, I took the final mouthful of the drink Jacie had made me.

Deep down, I knew this shit was already on a path that was gonna spiral outta control. While Animal was riding his high, he could do anything. The fact none of the brothers had followed him inside after their earlier trash talk meant no one else was actually gonna play his game. But that was of little comfort. Especially with how my need to keep Jacie protected grew with every passing minute. I probably should just say something to Viper and Scout. Let the two presidents deal with this situation. But that'd have me branded a rat, something I'd never been. It would also have me cut out of the loop from that point on.

And I wasn't allowing that to happen. Not for a second. Anything that might be a threat to Jacie was something I needed to know about. Because that woman was mine to protect.

At least, she was gonna be. And soon.

Chapter 3

Jacie

Sipping the last of my Old Fashioned, I kept my gaze on the guy who'd zeroed in on Trident. From the moment the large man had come storming out of the hallway, the hairs on the back of my neck had risen. That bloke was trouble, and not the fun kind.

He scanned the room and when his dark gaze zeroed in on me, my breath stilled in my lungs at the crazed look in his eyes. He was either high or unstable. Or maybe both. Without looking away, I set my empty glass down on the table. If I was going to have to make a run for it, I'd need to be bloody fast about it. While I technically knew how to take the guy down, he was a big bastard. And if he was hopped up on drugs, it was safer to get away rather than tackle him head on. Especially when I knew I only had to make it to the rear yard for back-up. Then Trident's dark eyes focused on me with a hard glint in them that had me clenching my jaw. As much as I hadn't caught a vibe earlier that he'd meant me harm, I couldn't be sure he'd back me up if shit went sideways with his club brother.

When the men turned to glare at each other and started talking too low for me to hear, I quickly glanced around the room in hopes a few Charons had snuck in. But I wasn't that lucky. Internally cursing my timing on needing some alone time to drink and lick my wounds, I shuffled over and out of the booth, moving silently deeper into the shadows, staying close to the wall as I headed toward a doorway. Reaching behind me, I pushed on the handle, but it didn't budge. Of course, it was locked. Dammit.

While monitoring both the men and the rest of the room, I continued to quietly move toward the second hallway, the one that led back to the club's offices. Surely, I'd be able to find one that was open that I could lock myself in while I decided my next move.

Seconds felt like hours as I crept my way around the perimeter of the room, holding my breath in anticipation of the men spotting me. When I made it down the hallway enough to be out of sight, I nearly tripped over my own damn feet in relief as I sucked in a few deep breaths. But I wasn't safe yet and wouldn't be until I was locked inside an office.

I nearly laughed when I struck gold on the third door I tried. At least I did until I'd rushed inside and shut the door. That was when I realized my luck wasn't so great after all. There was no fucking lock! Closing my eyes, I pinched the bridge of my nose. What should I do? Going back out into the open hallway didn't seem like a great idea, but if they caught me in here, it would be even worse. I could call Taz, but then he'd come raging in here on the warpath and end up causing some massive thing between the two clubs. And while I was still learning about how MCs worked, I'd been told more than once that it was vital that the Charons stay on the SCMC's good side.

Chewing on my lower lip, I hoped that me bitching out Trident earlier hadn't already ruined that. Surely not? I couldn't be the first woman to put a SCMC bloke in his place. And anyhow, I wasn't wearing a Charon patch. Any insult would be from me personally, not the club. I groaned. That was worse! Surely, Taz and the club would still have my back though, right? I was his sister, a blood relative.

Deciding my personal safety trumped inter-club politics, I went for my phone. I'd just tapped the screen, lighting it up, when a shadow covered the upper glass half of the door. Then, before I could react, it slammed open, causing me to drop my phone with a squeal as I jumped back out of the strike zone.

Trident filled the doorway, looking way larger than he had when he'd been sitting at the bar. And the look on his face was nothing like the one he'd given me then either. Gone was the jokester I'd been bantering with, or even the hard-ass biker who'd been arguing with his club brother, and in its place was a stone-faced soldier. Without looking away from me, he ducked down and scooped up my phone from where I'd dropped it and slipped it into his pocket faster than I could voice a protest. When he then lunged toward me, I instinctively lifted a palm while I backed away, only stopping when I hit the wall and couldn't go any further. He kept coming until my palm was against his chest, over his name patch. He slapped one hand against the wall beside my head, while the other he wrapped around the front of my throat, squeezing enough to have me gasping out a breath, but not enough to have me full on panicking. Yet.

"Trying to run from me ain't ever gonna be a good idea, girlie. Never do that again. Especially when you got danger nipping at your heels. We need to get you somewhere safer than here. You got a place we can go to? Away from the clubhouse."

Of course, I did. He couldn't possibly think I actually lived here, a single woman not part of the club. With the hand not wedged between us, I reached up and tried to pry his fingers away from my throat, but he frustratingly didn't budge. Just raised his eyebrow as he watched me struggle.

Glaring his way, I growled out my words. "Yeah, I do, but again with that whole *I don't know you well enough* thing I mentioned earlier."

Jerking his hand away from my neck, he jabbed a finger toward the main bar. "That man who was checking you out like you were a juicy steak? He's currently high as a fucking kite and your brother's woman made a helluva fool outta him and some of my other brothers a while back. Animal's been pretty vocal about wanting revenge ever since, but old ladies are off limits. Especially pregnant ones. You however, ain't wearing a patch. He seems to think that makes it open season on you. That leaves you with limited options. You can call your big bro, which I'm guessing you were about to do, and we can sit back and watch him and Animal go at it. Not sure who'll win, to be honest. Your brother has a rep that once he loses his cool, he's near unstoppable. Issue is, Animal has the same damn rep. And he's got poison in his veins to hype him up. You want Taz hurt? Be responsible for a rift between the clubs that'll fuck us all over? Or you wanna help me help you and tell me somewhere I can fuckin' take you so I can keep you safe tonight?"

The blood had drained from my head while he'd spoken, as I'd imagined what he'd described playing out. It could absolutely happen as he'd said. I cleared my throat as I tried to get my spinning thoughts to make sense. He'd spoken the truth, I didn't doubt that. One unpatched woman was not worth all that chaos he'd just described, and while Taz was strong and had been in the USMC, he had slacked off since Flick got pregnant again. She'd struggled with morning sickness, so Taz had stepped up to do more around the house and with Lolly, their eldest daughter. That had meant less time for workouts and training sessions. There was no way he was in peak condition. He certainly didn't have the added fuel of drugs in his system.

"I don't want to stir up trouble for anyone, but I also don't want to risk leading any member of your club to where I live if so many of them want to see me hurt."

I might live above Athena Security, which meant my place had a state-of-the-art system on it, but that wouldn't stop a bunch of bikers from breaking in. They'd be able to do a lot of damage before anyone could make it to me if they came during the night.

Pain and anger flashed in his eyes as though I'd struck him. "Have I given you even the *slightest* hint that I would ever harm you? I'm currently breaking one of my club's top rules for you, for fuck's sake. 'Brothers First, Brothers Forever'."

I shook my head. "Don't start lying to me now. You just told me you're basically preventing an inter-club war by guarding me. That's your top reason for being here. As you also pointed out, I'm nothing. An unpatched female at a club party."

A dark, low chuckle that held no humor echoed around me. The deep rumble of it vibrated from his chest through to my hand that was still pressed up against his solid left pec, which sent completely inappropriate spikes of arousal through me.

"You that oblivious, babe?" He shook his head before muttering, "Thinks she's nothing."

Moving quickly, he had both of my wrists in one of his hands and pinned to the wall above my head. Then he pressed his front flush against me, the heat rolling off him nearly scolding me as he ground against me, the thick, hard length of him obvious as he rubbed it over my belly. "Let me be crystal fucking clear. I want you, Jacie. Ain't just doing this for my club. You've caught my interest, babe. Never gonna lie about that. And you're lying to yourself if you think Taz and his club wouldn't do everything they could to protect you. That's where it'll get messy. While the Charons won't care you're not patched, Animal does. He'll use that to convince our president to back him to suffer no retaliation for what he'll do to you."

I only managed to hear about half of what he said, because with him grinding his pelvis against mine, my blood had gone from ice to lava within a few heartbeats. I knew it was mostly my adrenaline needing somewhere to go, but I couldn't seem to stop myself.

Struggling to suck in breaths, I arched my back, pressing my breasts more firmly into his chest, while I tried to tug my hands free. With a curse, he dropped my wrists, and I wrapped my arms around his neck, scraping my nails through the buzzed hair above his nape while I tilted my hips up against his, earning myself a groan from him before he shoved both of his hands into my hair, gripping tight fists full to tug my head back, then his lips crashed down over mine, and time stopped.

All my nerve endings came alive as he kissed me. His tongue licked over my lower lip, demanding entry, and with a moan, I opened up under him. With a growl, he deepened the kiss, thrusting his tongue in and out in such a way that sent a rush of heat flooding my knickers. When I lowered my hands from his neck, he moved away enough to give me space to explore. Slipping under his cut to his bare skin, I mapped out his hard, smooth pecs with my fingertips. When I brushed over his tight little nipples, I paused to tweak them, earning me a sexy growl before he bit down on my lower lip, tugging it before ending our kiss.

Panting for breath, I looked up to take in his flushed face.

"Fuck me, we shouldn't be doing this but hell if I can resist you."

Before I could do more than blink, I found myself slung over his shoulder as he marched out into the hallway. I tried to wriggle around to ease the pressure of his shoulder against my stomach, but he simply wrapped a strong arm over my thighs, trapping me to him, without missing a step. Bracing my hands on his waist, I pushed my head up so I could see my surroundings. As he strode through the main room, I scanned the area, grateful it was still empty. Guess the prospect who'd been at the bar had decided against returning to his post at all. But more importantly, there were no SCMC members to report back to Animal or follow us. When he started up the stairs, I stiffened, realizing he must be planning on taking me up to one of the bedrooms. Another totally inappropriate wave of heat flashed between my thighs, and I clenched them together in a vain attempt to ease the ache.

At least the bedrooms all had solid locks on them. And if he kissed me again like he had in the office, I might be able to forget about how big of a bastard he could be and get lucky on my birthday, after all.

A shudder ran through me when he pressed his nose against my butt and inhaled.

"Fuck, you smell good. You want me too, dontcha? You're burning so hot for me, I can feel the heat through the leather of my cut."

Not bothering to even attempt to deny his claim, I

let my head fall down, releasing the strain on my neck, squeezing my eyes closed when he began to rub his thumb firmly over the seam of my jeans that ran between my thighs. After a few minutes, I was nearly mindless with arousal, and couldn't help but thrust against his shoulder, desperate for more friction for what I needed to go over the edge.

Slipping my palms into his rear pockets, I squeezed his firm ass, wishing we were naked.

"Dammit, woman. Give me a fuckin' minute, and I'll get you taken care of."

He sped up until he was nearly jogging by the time he reached the upper-level hallway, proving he'd stayed here before, not slowing until he got to a door that was open. Storming in, he kicked the door shut then set me on my feet beside it.

"Stay put for a sec."

He flipped the lock on the door, but that clearly wasn't enough for him because he snatched the wooden chair from the desk and wedged it under the handle, testing it wouldn't budge before he turned to scan the room with his serious soldier expression from earlier firmly in place. Goose bumps rose on my arms. Frowning, I rubbed my palms over them as the arousal that had been sizzling in my veins a moment ago cooled.

Watching him prowl around the small room, I wondered what the hell he was doing. Well, I mean it was obvious he was searching for any threats, but why? Aside from the Athena Security office, the Charon MC clubhouse was about the safest place in Bridgewater. With sure, fast movements, he moved around, opening and closing every cupboard and drawer before he disappeared into the bathroom. When he returned moments later, his gaze zeroed in on me, and with a head tilt, he cocked that eyebrow of his at me again.

"Situational awareness, babe. Always know exactly what's around you. Where the exits are. No matter how distracted you are. Never know when things will go FUBAR."

Bloody military types and their love of acronyms.

"You gotta speak English, T. FUBAR?"

He chuckled as he strode toward me, backing up against the wall.

"Like that you're already givin' me your own nickname, *Ula'ula Mō'ī*. FUBAR means something is fucked up beyond all recognition."

That had me grinning. "I need to remember that one. Could come in handy."

I wanted to ask him what the hell had happened to him to be so hardcore about safety and for a translation of whatever he'd just called me. But before I could say a word, he began to strip off his cut, which had me forgetting all about my questions. My earlier arousal sparked back to life as I sighed in appreciation. The man was a work of art.

Chapter 4

Trident

I wasn't exactly known for being a man who smiled much. Quite the opposite, in fact. But around this woman, I seemed to be grinning more often than not. Without taking my gaze off her, I stepped to the side to place my jewelry and cut on the desk, then took both our phones out of my pocket and set them down next to my cut before returning to stand in front of her.

I might be forty-one years old, but I'd kept up my training since leaving the Marines. The main reason for that was safety, so I'd always be able to keep me and mine protected, but it had the side benefit of leaving me being easy on the eyes. At least that's what a whole lot of women had told me over the years, but none of them had ever done to me what Jacie's sweet little sigh and glazed eyes had done just now. My cock wasn't just aching, it was throbbing in the confines of my jeans.

In the back of my mind, a warning alarm started blaring, but I shut that shit down real fast, ignoring it for probably the first time since I'd been a teen. This little Aussie spitfire had me hooked good and I needed to taste her, get inside her, so fucking bad. Now that I'd confirmed the room was secure and knew the door was as locked as I could get it, I intended to spend the rest of the evening and night fully focused on her. By morning I'd know every inch of her intimately, and she'd know who she fucking belonged to.

I couldn't fucking wait.

With my hands on her waist, I nuzzled my face in against her neck, loving how her pale skin reddened from my beard rubbing over it. Also loved that she liked it enough that she tilted her head to the side, giving me more room as she lifted her palms to rest on my hips. Moving down, I nipped at her collarbone, and in response, she scraped her short nails up over the ridges of my abs, which had me shuddering as spears of arousal shot through my system, making me desperate for more of her.

Gripping the bottom of her tight little t-shirt, I pulled it up and over her head in one smooth move. My gaze zeroed in on her tits as I tossed the fabric in my hands aside. The black satin cupping her soft mounds had a lacy edge and was sexy as fuck, but it was in my way, so it had to go. Running my tongue over my lower lip, I slipped a palm around her ribcage then up her spine until I hit the clasp, which I flipped open in seconds with a well-practiced move. Then I made short work of sending her bra to the floor to join her shirt. Tight, dusty-pink tips topped her perky tits, and I couldn't wait to test how sensitive she was there. How responsive she'd be to my touch.

When she started to move her arms to cover herself, I shook my head on a growl.

"No way, don't you dare hide yourself from me. You're fucking gorgeous, and I'm gonna do a helluva lot more than just look by the time we're through here."

Then, before she could take another breath, I had my lips over hers, devouring her mouth as I got my hands on her sweet tits. She was small enough that my palms completely covered them, her hard nipples scraping over my skin as I caressed and kneaded her breasts. When she started squirming, pushing into my hands, I began to pinch at her tight tips before rolling them between my thumbs and forefingers, then gently twisting them. I continued to eat at her mouth as she whimpered and dug her fingertips into my waist, while I continued to torment her. Loving that she was proving to be everything I'd hoped she'd be, sensitive and responsive to the edge of roughness I needed to dish out. I didn't stop until she tore her lips from mine to cry out, her fingers digging in hard enough I knew she'd leave marks, if not draw blood with her nails, even with them being short.

Releasing her nipples, I shuffled away half a step and glanced down, my dick twitching at the sight of her now ruby-red nipples. Desperation for her clouded my mind as I reached for the waistband of her jeans. Attacking the fly, fumbling in my haste, I growled. Her quiet chuckle had me pausing to look into her face to appreciate how fucking gorgeous she was with her eyes sparkling with humor and arousal.

Leaning in, she pressed a light kiss to the corner of my mouth as she slipped her hands under mine to undo the button and lower the zipper. Splaying my hand over her flat stomach, teasing my fingers over the sensitive skin just above her panties, I kept my gaze locked on hers as she shuddered, and her lids lowered.

"Trident, quit teasing me already."

"Babe, I'm only just getting started."

With that, I tugged the sides of her jeans down so

they were around her hips, keeping her legs together, then shoved my hand down into her lacy black panties. My knees went a little weak while I groaned at what I found.

"Fuck, babe, you're bare."

She stiffened. "Hope you like it, T, because I'm lasered. That hair's never growing back."

I dropped my head onto her shoulder. She couldn't tell I fucking loved it?

"Yeah, *Ula'ula Mō'ī*, it's fucking perfect."

I'd already wanted to get my mouth on her, but now that I knew there'd be nothing between my lips and tongue and her skin? I couldn't fucking wait. But I would. For a little longer, at least. Sliding my fingers over her smooth mound, I kept going between her slick folds to her entrance where I thrust my middle finger in deep. With her jeans as they were, she was extra tight, but she was wet enough that I slid easily in and out of her channel. Using my other hand to cup one of her tits, I kneaded the flesh before holding it up so I could lower my mouth and suckle on the tip, pausing every so often to use my tongue to tease the tight bud as I finger-fucked her until she was bucking against me and moaning in frustration.

"More, T. I need more."

Switching to her other breast, I slid my fingers all the way out of her pussy, making sure to graze over her clit before lowering once more, and pushing two fingers into her core this time. I made a point to target her G-spot by curling my fingers every time I thrust into her.

She was so fucking slick and needy, rolling her hips against me with my every stroke, riding my fingers like she would my cock. The wet suction sounds coming from her pussy were deliciously filthy. That, together with her moans and whimpers, filled the room with the best symphony I'd ever heard, one I'd never tire of hearing. When the ache in my cock grew too insistent to ignore, I released her breast and slipped my hand from her panties, making sure to brush over her clit again as I did, loving how she jerked at the teasing contact.

"Need you naked, babe."

Not wanting to miss a moment, I kept my gaze on her as I stepped away to give her some room. Once she'd kicked off her shoes and had begun to lower her pants, I toed off my boots and nearly tore the denim in my rush to get my fly undone.

Blowing out a breath, I forced myself to slow the fuck down and look at what I was doing for a few moments. Then with steady fingers, I got the button and zipper dealt with. Looping my thumbs under the waistband of both my jeans and boxer-briefs, I shoved them down my legs, kicking them free before tugging off my socks and tossing them aside with everything else.

As I straightened, my gaze zeroed in on her, as though she were a magnet or something. My heart skipped a damn beat at the sight she made, her perfect white teeth pressed down into her lush pink lower lip while she stared at my cock. Seemed as though she'd stalled out, hands gripping the sides of her panties, the only thing she was now wearing. Had to say, this woman did wonders for my ego. What man didn't want his woman pausing in wonder when she first saw his dick? Gripping my hard length in my palm, I started slowly stroking myself, grinning as her eyes followed the movement.

"Keep going, babe. Need to see that pretty pussy of yours that I'll be fillin' up real soon."

Tilting her head back against the wall with a loud

exhale, she closed her eyes and clenched her hands into fists around the fabric she held.

"I shouldn't be here. Shouldn't find your demanding bullshit such a fucking turn-on."

Releasing my cock, I stepped toward her. With one hand pressed against the wall beside her head, I leaned in until I could brush my nose against hers, teasing her with a barely there touch. Then with my other hand, the one that'd been on my dick a few moments ago, I rubbed over her panties. She pressed her palms against my chest, having me worried I'd misread things. I paused to see if she'd shove me away, to put more space between us, when she didn't, I got back to what I was doing, pushing the soaked fabric against her flesh until it molded over her bare mound and pussy lips. Her clit was so fucking hard, I could feel the little nub through the thin fabric. Scraping a nail over it a few times, I enjoyed how she jerked at each pass, how her blue irises, that were locked on mine, glazed over with bliss. When her mouth opened as she started panting for breath, I pressed my thumb between her folds as deep as the fabric would allow while I shifted my head to the side so I could nip at her earlobe.

"You're the one bullshitting us both if you think you don't want this. Want me. Your panties are soaked. Reckon I'll have you comin' in seconds once I get my mouth on this hot little pussy of yours, then again even harder once I get my dick in you."

My words left her shuddering, groaning as she tilted her hips up against me, seeking more friction while her fingers curled into my pecs. Yeah, she wanted everything I was gonna give her. After delivering one more nip to her earlobe, I pulled my hand from between her thighs and gripped the front of her neck. Holding her still so I could give her another rough kiss. Without removing my lips from hers, I lowered both hands to her panties, gripping the thin fabric over her hip before giving it a sharp tug, ripping the fabric. Before her mind could fully comprehend what I was doing, I moved to the other side and did the same thing before peeling the wet fabric away from her and tossing it aside. I'd make sure I grabbed them later... they were mine now.

Breaking the kiss, I returned my palm to her throat then pressed my knee between her thighs, raising it until I could feel her slick pussy sliding against me.

"Trident..."

She dragged out my name as she moved her hands down and around to my waist and started grinding against my leg.

"Yeah, that's it, babe. Be a good girl and ride me. Fuck, I can't wait to do all sorts of wicked things to you."

Lowering my hand from her throat, I gave her right nipple a pinch and twist while nuzzling my face into her neck, rubbing my beard over her sensitive skin until she was whimpering and her movements against my leg had grown jerky. Releasing her tit, I dropped to my knees. The slaps of her palms against the wall were loud in the room as I threw one of her legs over my shoulder. The hitch in her breath when I spread her bare lips open with my thumbs and blew over her wet folds had my dick throbbing. Leaning in, I delivered one long lick from as far back as I could reach up until I could tease her hard little clit.

"Bloody hell, T!"

Chuckling at her cursing, I took a moment to savor my first taste of her. Fuck, her musky sweetness was perfection, and I wanted—no, needed—more.

She rolled her hips with a whimper, and I focused back on my mission to have her mindless from all the orgasms I was gonna give her. Teasing her inner thigh with my beard, I chuckled when she cursed again, enjoying the hell out of how fucking responsive she was to my every touch.

"You taste so fucking good, Jacie. I'm gonna wanna eat you for breakfast, lunch and dinner, seven days a week."

She shook her head and opened her mouth like she was gonna tell me some bullshit about this being for just one night, but before she could utter a word, I covered her wet, pink slit with my mouth and plunged my tongue deep into her channel. Thrusting in and out, I moved a thumb up to her clit, rubbing small circles on the tight bud until she shuddered then blew apart for me, calling my name.

Sweetest fucking sound I'd ever heard? My name on her lips as she came. I couldn't wait to hear it again. That voice in the back of my mind whispered that it'd be even sweeter to hear her calling out my real name, but that shit could shut the fuck up. No one called me by my birth name anymore. I doubted many in the club even knew what it was.

Moving my hand away from her now over-sensitive clit, I wrapped my palm around my twitching cock as, with a hum, I ate up all the cream she was giving me. I'd always fucking loved going down on a woman. Being surrounded by her musk as I made her shatter again and again for me. Making sure she was well and truly slick enough that when I fucked her, I could slam in deep on the first stroke. But I'd never enjoyed it as much as I was right now, with Jacie. There was just something about this woman that got to me. And I couldn't fucking wait to get inside her, fill her up. Claim her as my own.

When she started to tremble, I gently lowered her leg so she had both feet on the ground when I stood.

Then before she could guess what I was up to, I pressed my shoulder against her stomach and lifted her.

"What the hell? Again with this?"

I shrugged the shoulder she wasn't on. "Fastest way to get you where I need you, babe."

Laying her out on the bed, my hand dropped back down to stroke my cock as I took in the sight she made. Flushed chest and face, her pale red, wavy hair spread out over the steel gray covers. She was staring at my dick again while she chewed on that lower lip of hers like she had earlier. My attention went lower when she clenched her thighs together before rubbing them against each other. Looked like my little hellcat wanted more, which was a damn good thing because I had plenty more to give her.

"Want your hands on your tits, babe, while you spread your legs wide for me. I'm not nearly done with you."

Her hands trembled as she slid them slowly up over her chest, until they covered her perky breasts. She was biting down on her lip so hard, it was a wonder she hadn't drawn blood, but the flush to her cheeks and sparkle in her gaze told me she was into what I was dishing out.

"Don't go hiding yourself from me, Jacie. Never try to do that. I wanna see your fingers on your sweet pink nipples, twisting and tugging on them until you're squirming."

Heat flared in her eyes. "And what are you planning on doing? Gonna stand there and jack off?"

I grinned as I chuckled at her sass.

"Nah, babe. As soon as you're a good girl and do what I say, I'm gonna make another meal outta you."

"Dammit, Trident."

As she groaned out the words, she squeezed her

thighs together and closed her eyes before she tilted her head back, revealing the long line of her pale neck. Which left me running my tongue over my lower lip as I mentally mapped out exactly where I'd mark her later, sucking on her sensitive skin until I left a strawberry that would tell every fucking man who saw her that she was claimed.

Chapter 5

Jacie

This bloke was going to drive me crazy. He'd already made me come once with his mouth and he wanted to do it again? Had I caught myself the mythical beast of an orally fixated man? Shifting my hands so my fingers were wrapped around my tender nipples, I squeezed both until my back arched and my legs fell open on their own accord.

"That's it, babe. Fuck, so damn pretty. I like that you're bare, can see exactly how wet you are for me. Get every drop of your cream."

Releasing the monster he'd been tugging on, he reached for my ankles and pulled me toward him, until my arse was near the edge of the mattress.

"Feet up."

He guided each leg until my feet rested with my heels up tight against my butt but spread wide enough I could feel the air of the room against my core. He dropped to his knees and with a palm on either side, he used his thumbs to spread me open, like he had earlier, but now he had more room. After smirking up at me, he blew a steady stream of air over my folds and exposed clit, that was still sensitive after my last orgasm.

"Don't forget about those tits, babe. Don't wanna have to stop to remind you. Want you teasing them until they're so sensitive, when I rub my beard over them later you'll come from that alone."

A shudder rocked through me at his words and he laughed, low and deep, while he leaned in and stroked that talented tongue of his through my folds, stabbing in deep before curling up and brushing over just the right spot.

"Trident!"

Knowing he'd struck gold, he kept teasing the spot with his tongue for a minute before he pulled out and wrapped those soft lips of his around my clit. I jerked when he first made contact, which resulted in me tugging hard on my nipples. The flash of pain mixed with my arousal making me groan as I cupped my breasts, pressing against my tender tips with some care now. I'd always had sensitive nipples and they were even more so now. I knew tomorrow that my every move would have my bra brushing over them and reminding me of tonight.

He slid two fingers easily into my core as he kept suckling on my clit. I tilted my hips, wanting more, and he delivered, adding a third digit as he continued to finger-fuck me. On each withdrawal, he spread his fingers apart, stretching me and delivering a delicious burn with each stroke that had me spiraling closer to climax.

I'd been a little shocked when I'd first seen his cock. Fully erect, he was long and thick. Larger than any other man I'd been with, and I couldn't wait to feel him deep within me. Just thinking about how well he'd fill me up had me spasming with a mini climax, my walls clamping down on his invading fingers. Moving his lips to my inner thigh, with a growl, he took a mouthful of flesh. Then before I could guess what he had planned, he sucked hard, marking me, as he jammed what had to be four fingers into my still quivering channel, his thumb grazing over my sensitized clit on each thrust.

Throwing my hands out, I gripped fists full of bedding as my back arched off the mattress. The burn of his fingers stretching me, the sting of his mouth marking my thigh, the barely there touches on my hyper sensitive clit, it all added to the fire boiling within me. After several strokes, he pulled free and returned with only two fingers. I whimpered at the loss until he curled them up and rubbed back and forth over my g-spot. My every muscle tightened as pleasure flooded my system.

"That's it, *Ula'ula Mŏ'ī.*"

I writhed on the bed, caught between wanting more and trying to escape. His beard tickled my other thigh a moment before his lips made contact, sucking on my skin to mark me as he'd done the other side earlier and the pain sent my pleasure sky high. Shattering apart, I cried out as I came so bloody hard my ears rung and my vision blacked out.

Blinking rapidly, I licked my lips and worked on getting my eyes to focus on Trident. Reaching my arms out for him, he grinned down at me, but didn't lean in straight away. He grabbed that thick erection of his, lined the head up with my opening and before I could utter a word, he slammed in all the way to the root.

"Fuck!"

My back arched again as my entire being shuddered at the invasion. He pulled slowly out before he thrust back inside me, deep. My core rippled around him, an aftershock of my previous orgasm. With a moan, he paused, his cock twitching within me. He was so damn big, filling me completely — even with how wet he'd gotten me, with how he'd stretched me, it still burned. My eyes watered but I didn't want him to stop. This wasn't simply pain, this was something more. Something I'd never felt and didn't know how to describe: yes, there was a sting each time he forced his way inside me, a burn as he slid in deep. But it didn't *hurt* — the sensation mixed with my arousal and adrenaline from earlier and I knew it wouldn't take him long to have me coming again.

"Fuck, babe, you're so damn tight. Can't get enough."

He dropped down over me on his next thrust in, and I wrapped my arms around his neck as his hands landed on the mattress on either side of me. His lips crashed against mine, kissing me roughly as he continued to move inside me. When I moaned, he deepened the kiss, thrusting his tongue in to dance with mine. A shudder ran through me as I tasted my musk on him. It was so fucking dirty but so damn good. Tilting my pelvis up, I ground against him, circling my hips so I could feel every inch of him inside me. Biting my lower lip, he gave it a tug before he pushed himself up and grinned down at me, a sparkle in his eyes I'd not seen before.

"You hungry for more, *Ula'ula Mõ'ī?*"

I wanted to know what that meant, but I'd worry about it later, because just then he moved us to the edge of the bed so he could stand. Keeping his hard length buried deep within me, he grabbed my left leg and moved it until my ankle rested on his right shoulder.

"Wrap your other leg around my waist, babe."

Desperate for more of him, I had my right leg around his lean hip almost before he'd finished speaking. Then, with a wicked smirk on his sexy face, he leaned forward. His left fist hit the mattress beside me to hold his weight up just high enough for him to get his other hand on my tits. Tweaking each nipple before pinching and twisting them until arousal had me dizzy.

"Trident!"

"That's right, babe. Gonna send you to the fuckin' moon."

When he released my breasts and planted his right hand on the bed beside me, he lowered his torso which pushed my legs further apart. The muscles up the back of my left thigh burned with the new angle but it was easy to ignore when he started moving that thick dick of his again. Wrapping my palms around his biceps to anchor myself, I gave myself over to him. A rag-doll he could move however he wanted. After he pumped slowly in and out of me several times, he lifted up enough to ease the strain on my muscles. Pausing, he ran his scorching hot gaze from my face, down my body to where we were joined. I lifted my head to follow his lead. With only the head of his cock inside me, I whimpered at the sight of his thick erection, shiny with my juices, ready to fill me once more. Anticipation had a rush of liquid heat blooming in my core a moment before he slammed deep inside again.

I cried out when he rubbed over my g-spot on each thrust in. Within seconds, bliss had me dropping my head back onto the bed and closing my eyes, I dug my fingers into the muscles of his forearms, and my heel into his tight ass, as he set about fucking me deep and hard with fast thrusts.

When he slowed down, I opened my eyes to look up into his face, getting caught in his sexy as fuck dark brown irises that I could happily drown in. Biting my lip, I arched my back, thrusting my breasts up. My nipples ached, throbbed with arousal and I wanted nothing more than to have his mouth suckling on them again. His gaze dropped to my offering and, with a growl, he straightened between my thighs. My hands fell to the bed where I gripped fists full of the sheets while I moaned at how good his cock felt twitching deep within me as he lowered my leg off his shoulder, guiding it until I wrapped it around his waist like my other one had already been.

"Lock your ankles together, babe."

Wondering what he was gonna do, I followed his instructions. As soon as I did, he leaned forward and pressed his lips against mine. I wrapped my arms around his neck and continued to kiss him while his palms slid underneath me: one cupping my ass while the other went between my shoulder blades. Breaking the kiss, I squealed when he lifted me. Trident buried his face into my neck — kissing, nipping, using his beard to tickle me as he walked away from the bed. With each step his cock moved in interesting ways that had me tightening my thigh muscles and grinding down on his length. His chuckle was deep and gravelly and had my body responding with a fresh flood of liquid.

"Fuck, you're perfect, *Ula'ula Mö'ı*. Unlink your ankles, and hold on to my shoulders for a minute."

He moved quickly to get my legs over his arms before gripping my waist in his palms. Then he stepped forward until my back hit a wall. I arched away from the cool surface and with a growl, he leaned down to lick over my nipples. Suckling each one a moment before he straightened and briefly took my mouth again.

Then his hips started to move and my brain short-circuited. Holy smokes, this position had me open wide to his invasion. His thrusts took him even deeper, his cock-head touching my cervix each time he bottomed out. The sting of pain with each tap sent a thrill through me that left my head rolling back and forth against the wall, my fingers slipping in the sweat coating his skin until I dug my nails into his upper biceps as I tried to hang on, to find something to anchor myself in the storm that was Trident.

He went wild on me, pounding at a rough pace I'd never have thought I'd like, but did. Well, I didn't just *like* it, I fucking loved it. Trident was ruining me for any other man but that didn't matter, not when another climax was building within me.

"So fuckin' good. I'm not gonna last long, but you're comin' with me, *Ula'ula Mõ'ī.*"

Without losing his rhythm, he released my right leg, lowering it until my foot was on the floor, then his hand dove between us, going straight for my clit. He flicked and pinched at it as he kept driving in deep, no longer bottoming out but that didn't make it any less powerful. Every stroke in had my walls rippling around him, every touch to my clit had my pulse increasing. Sweat slicked my body, running down between my breasts as I panted, chanting his name.

"Now, babe. Come for me right fucking now!"

With that he slammed in hard, holding himself deep. His cock kicked within me and warmth bloomed as he filled me up. Panic flared inside me as I realized he hadn't worn a bloody condom. At least it did until he distracted me by pinching my clit as he buried his face in against my neck, the brush of his beard over my flesh mixed with the arousal already spiraling within me and my mind emptied of everything but him. The pleasure he was drowning me with. When he turned his face and sucked on the skin just above my collarbone, marking me, it was enough to push me over the edge. Sending me flying to the stars with how hard I orgasmed.

Moaning, I woke to an aching body. What the bloody hell had happened? Had I been in a car accident or something? Then flashes of memory began rolling through my mind and heat flared between my thighs and my hips tilted forward, my core wanting to be filled again.

Biting my lip to stop a groan from escaping, I peeked through lowered lashes to see if Trident was still beside me. The moonlight streaming in through the window spotlit him. Fucking hell, even in his sleep he looked all masculine and sexy as fuck. How was I meant to resist? We hadn't pulled the covers up after our last round so he lay sprawled out on his back, one leg out at an angle and his dick laid against it. Even soft, he was big. I bit my lip even harder, until I tasted blood, in order to resist the urge I suddenly had to lean down and take him in my mouth. To feel him harden against my tongue before I straddled him and slid down that delicious length and rode him.

No. Bad Jacie. Bikers are off the menu. Last night was a one off. No repeats.

That made me sigh, because dammit, I sorta wanted to break my rule about bikers that I'd only made last night. Trident let out a small snore and I snapped out of my daydream. I needed to be gone from here before he woke. While I had spent much of the previous night mindless, I did recall all the possessive shit he'd said to me. Along with the fact that he hadn't used a single condom. I kept meaning to bring it up, but then he'd get his hands, or mouth, on me and my brain would shut down. I couldn't risk that happening again this morning. Thankfully, I was on the pill, but that didn't prevent diseases. I slipped from the bed as carefully and quietly as I could. Looking around I spotted my jeans, bra and shirt but no knickers. The increasing amount of moisture coating my inner thighs now that I'd stood up meant going commando wasn't an option. Seeing Trident's boxer-briefs, I snagged those along with my clothes and rushed over to the bathroom. After a quick clean up and making a pad out of loo paper to soak things up, I dressed and finger combed back my hair. It was a curly chaotic mess, and I couldn't do much with it right now, but I did what I could.

Stepping back into the main room, I took in Trident one last time. Still fast asleep, snoring quietly. Man was a work of art, and damn, did he know exactly how to use that fabulous dick of his. And his tongue. And his fingers. Shaking my head, I scolded myself again and headed to the door. No matter how tempting it was to go crawl into bed with him again, I couldn't do it. Nope. I was not going to be the property of some biker. No matter how hot, or how good at blowing my mind, he was.

Slipping out into the hallway, I looked both ways, relieved to see it was clear. I tiptoed down to the room I'd left my stuff in last night, where I'd originally intended to sleep, and unlocked the door. Thankfully, the key had stayed put in my jeans pocket. I rushed to get inside and the door locked behind me. Then I leaned back against it and closed my eyes on a sigh.

What the fuck had I done last night? Unprotected sex with a stranger! A much older, sexy biker of a one-percenter club who no doubt fucked all sorts of skanky women without gloving up. Now I was going to have to go get tested. It would take fucking months before I'd know if I'd avoided catching any nasties. Not exactly the birthday present I'd been hoping for. At least I was on the Pill, along with it being the wrong time of the month, so I didn't need to stress about pregnancy.

Scrubbing my hands over my face, I felt like

screaming into them. But I resisted the urge, not wanting to risk drawing attention from anyone who might be in the rooms beside mine. With a tired sigh, I walked over to my bag and grabbed the large shirt I'd brought to sleep in, some knickers and my toiletries bag before heading to the bathroom.

A hot shower was what I needed to clear my head and hopefully ease some of my aches, not that I was complaining. I'd thoroughly enjoyed earning every one of them. Which was a problem because I'd liked it so much, I wasn't sure I'd be able to resist going another round with Trident if we crossed paths again. Although, with how I'd just snuck out on him, he might not even want to look at me, let alone anything more.

As I stepped under the spray, I decided avoiding him would be the easiest thing to do. I'd need to hide out here until the other club headed off before I could risk leaving. And I'd make sure if I ever came back to the Charon MC clubhouse, it wasn't when any of the SCMC brothers were going to be around.

Chapter 6

Trident

Since neither of us had thought to shut the curtains last night, when the sun rose enough to hit the window, the rays woke me. While I was not normally a fan of being blasted in the face with a bright light, I didn't mind it today, not when I had my little *Ula'ula Mõ'ī* beside me. Reaching down I gave my aching cock a stroke as I rolled over with a grin, ready to wake Jacie up in the best way.

"Are you fucking kidding me?"

Looked like my morning wood wouldn't get any relief, since I was fucking alone in the damn bed. Running my hand over the spot where she'd been, the cold sheets let me know she'd been gone a while. Shifting to sit on the edge of the bed left me staring through the open door to the clearly empty bathroom. The little coward had snuck off on me. She could think again if she thought I'd give up that easily. I'd claimed her last night. I never fucked a woman without gloving up unless I was making her mine. When I found my little runaway, I'd make sure she knew what being mine meant.

With a shake of my head, I went to the bathroom. If

she hadn't left me with an aching dick, I'd have been impressed at her stealth. Ever since going through USMC Hell Week, I'd woken at the slightest of noises. Seemed like several rounds of sex with Jacie had me sleeping like the dead.

Returning to the room, I snatched up my clothes and cursed again when I noticed what was missing.

"Damn woman."

Oh, she was gonna pay for this little stunt when I caught up with her. Taking a man's underwear was not okay, especially when said man was gonna have to ride for over five hours soon. I was well aware my woman would throw it in my face that I hadn't given her a choice, considering I'd torn hers up in my need to get her naked last night, but that was bullshit. If she hadn't up and ghosted me, I'd have made sure she was cleaned up and well taken care of before she left the room. Hell, she wouldn't have even remembered she was missing her damn panties by the time I'd gotten done with her.

After pulling up my jeans and carefully zipping them closed over my aching dick, I grabbed the scraps of her underwear and shoved them into my pocket. Wasn't gonna leave that behind. Shrugging into my cut, I put my jewelry on and tucked my phone and wallet away. Then I was out in the hallway, glancing both ways while I stroked a hand over my beard. Where would my little runaway be hiding? Her ride was a sweet black Harley Davidson Softail Breakout 114. I'd heard how loud that little beast could roar, and knew full well I'd have woken up, along with most of the others staying here, if she'd even tried to start it, let alone if she'd taken off on it.

With a sigh I headed toward the stairs. I couldn't go knocking on doors to find her. Last thing I needed this morning was Taz, or any of the other Charon brothers, up in my grill about my intentions or some other shit.

What was between me and Jacie was just that: between me and her. Once on the ground floor, it didn't take long to scan over everyone who'd crashed in the main room. It was nothing unusual to have folks sleeping all over the place after a big party. Some of the snoring men had club girls draped over them, while a couple were awake and putting their women to good use. Doing what I'd wanted to do to Jacie when I'd woken up earlier.

Lucky bastards.

As I passed the table where all of us SCMC brothers had dropped our shirts after we'd gotten in yesterday, I snatched mine out of the pile and tucked one end into my back pocket as I continued on my way. A quick trip down the hallway that led to the club's offices, where I'd found her last night, turned up nothing but silence and empty or locked rooms. Next I headed to the kitchen, where I found Stone sitting at the big center table, nursing a coffee.

"Morning, Trident." He ran his gaze over me. "Considering how early you disappeared last night, figured you'd be looking way more satisfied than you do this morning. You luck out or something?"

I ran a hand over my beard and gave it a tug as I contemplated how I should answer the man who wasn't just a fellow SCMC member; he was also Flick's biological brother. He raised an eyebrow my way.

"Cat got your tongue? If it helps, I was tailing Animal all day and night yesterday. Stayed out of sight, but I saw how you played hero to my brother-in-law's baby sis."

Fucker already knew I'd spent the night with Jacie. Glaring his way, I was about to rip into him, but he cut me off before I could.

"So long as you don't plan on hurtin' her, I ain't got a problem with you being with Jacie, but I will caution you to think it through before it gets serious. Animal's got a helluva hard on for her, and if you start bringing her around the clubhouse, waving her under his nose, shit'll get outta control fast."

Keeping my expression neutral took some effort. Because him warning me like that fucking stung. We'd known each other for a long time, so for him to think for even a moment that I'd knowingly cause any female harm was bullshit.

"You know me better than that, Stone. I wouldn't ever hurt any woman, especially not one I've claimed."

This conversation was making my already bad mood worse by the second. Since I'd have to ride back to Cutler soon, I couldn't self-medicate with alcohol. That left me with caffeine. Turning away from the table, I headed toward the row of pod machines to make myself the strongest coffee I could find.

"You already put her under your protection? Not sure that's wise, Trident. Not only does that girl have fucking trouble from our club after her, she's a wild one and loves her freedom about as much as any mustang I've ever seen. You think you're gonna be able to tame the untamable, brother? Because she's been very fucking vocal about not wanting to be patched by anyone. Drives Taz up the damn wall that she won't even accept a Charon Daughter of the Club cut."

With a shake of my head, I removed my drink from the machine now that it was done and took a mouthful before I turned to face him and leaned against the bench.

"That woman is mine. I made it crystal fucking clear to her last night that I was claiming her. Made sure I got her consent before I had her screaming my name."

He scoffed, humor lighting his eyes. "That so? Tell me, brother, was she not paying attention when you told her? Because you don't fucking look like a man who's just pinned down his old lady. Nor do I see her by your side this morning."

Bastard had to call me out.

"Fuck off, Stone. She got spooked this morning, is all. Soon as I find my little runaway, I'll set her straight. And Animal will back the fuck off now that I've claimed her. He knows better than to come after a brother's woman, especially mine."

Animal had tried to best me more than once in the past, and it had never ended well for him. Even before he fell into drugs, he kept thinking just because he was younger and an officer that meant he was the bigger man. He wasn't. The only reason I wasn't an officer was because I didn't fucking want to be one. I was happy being an enforcer. And with his recent escalating drug use, I doubted he'd be an officer for much longer. The SCMC needed a treasurer who could think straight with a clear enough mind to fucking count.

I cleared my throat, "So, ah, speaking of her whereabouts. I don't suppose you've seen her? Know where she'd be hiding?"

He laughed then, a dark chuckle that sounded strange coming from the man. He'd earned his road name because he'd been stone cold, never showing any emotion. At least, he had been until he and his sister reconnected a few years back. Since then, he'd come out of his shell, slowly becoming more human. We were all still getting used to this new version of him.

"Haven't seen her, man. But I doubt she's left the clubhouse. That bike of hers would've woken near everyone here if she'd ridden out, and I doubt she'd try to walk home. It's a bit of a hike from here, and if she had taken off on foot, she'd have sum' explaining to do later to her brother about why she left without her ride."

After taking another mouthful of coffee, I straightened and strode toward the door.

"I figured the same. She ain't hiding in an empty office like she was last night either. Ain't in here. Doubt she'd be out in the yard, but I'll go check."

Before I could make it out of the room, Stone called out again.

"Trident?"

"Yeah?"

He spoke as he stood, moving over to put his mug in the sink. "You know as well as I do, she's most likely in one of the rooms upstairs, which means you're shit outta luck. Because if you start knocking on doors, you'll have the whole Charon MC on your ass in a heartbeat. Listen, she ain't going anywhere anytime soon. Not only is she staying in Bridgewater to be near her brother and family, she's working for the Charons now, too. She's settled in well, but Taz has made it so no man is game to even look in her direction, so you got some time to lock her down."

He gave me a friendly clap on the shoulder as he passed me then headed toward the main room while I went the other way, out into the rear yard. Once outside it didn't take long to realize I was alone with nothing but some mess from the party that the prospects and club girls would no doubt clean up soon. Putting my mug down on the picnic table, I took off my cut, then grabbing my shirt from my pocket, put the thing on before I shrugged back into my colors.

Scanning the yard again, I shook my head. I knew Stone was right. My little runaway was being a coward and hiding in one of the upstairs rooms and I couldn't do a damn thing about it.

Dropping down to sit on the picnic table, I sipped at my brew as I tried to think of an excuse to return to

Bridgewater in the next few days. There was no way I was letting my little spitfire escape me for long. Didn't matter she hadn't given me her phone number or address.

That had me pausing with my mug at my lips.

"Motherfucker!"

Stone had said that it was too far for her to walk home; that meant he damn well knew where she lived. Climbing off the table, I was about to head inside when my phone dinged with an incoming message. Pulling the device out, I saw it was from Tank, the club's Sargent at Arms.

Rolling out in 10 for home. Be ready.

Guess I'd have to wait on grilling Stone for info until after we got back to Cutler.

Chapter 7

Jacie

I'd stayed hidden away until nearly lunchtime, making sure that not only had all the SCMC guys cleared out, but most of the Charons too. Then I'd slipped quietly downstairs and outside. After I'd managed to escape without anyone trying to talk to me, I'd been riding high thinking that I'd succeeded in keeping my clandestine night with a biker a secret. But as the sun set I realized I hadn't been that lucky after all.

My apartment above Athena Security, where I worked, had some advantages. Like the state of the art security system that meant I'd been able to watch my big bro from the moment he came roaring in on his bike, to when he stomped up the stairs to my door. Where he ignored the perfectly functioning doorbell and instead started pounding his fist on the thick timber.

With a sigh, I pulled open the door, and smiled sweetly at my frowning sibling.

"Hey Taz, whatcha doing in my neck of the woods? Wanna coffee? Beer? Vegemite and cheese sandwich maybe?"

His expression blanked for a moment before, with a

shake of his head, he was back to frowning while he pushed past me to enter my apartment.

"You and your fucking Vegemite sandwiches..."

The Aussie condiment that resembled black tar wasn't everyone's cup of tea. Mostly because they ate it wrong. It wasn't like peanut butter, you had to use a light hand. A small smear of that salty goodness over a thick slice of cheese on buttered bread was delicious perfection.

Ignoring his cursing, I shut and locked the door behind him. Mumbling under my breath as I did. "Come on in, Taz. Make yourself at home."

"Don't pull that shit with me, Jacie. Trying to distract me with a trip down memory lane ain't gonna save you. What the fuck happened last night after you left the rear yard? I couldn't find you after I got done with that bloody prospect. The ladies said you'd just gone inside for a drink, but you never came back. Me and Flick didn't see you inside when we headed home later either, but I sure as fuck noticed that your bike was still in the same spot this morning as it had been last night. So, what gives?"

As much as I'd known this confrontation was coming, I wasn't ready for it. It had been the main reason I'd been laying low all day today. Mind you, I could have had a month to come up with the perfect thing to say and it wouldn't have mattered. Not when my big bro was behaving like some sort of medieval throwback who thought he could control my every move just because he was born first and had a dick. That shit got my temper fired up like nothing else could. And when I got riled up like I currently was, anything I may have planned to say went straight out the window as my emotions took over.

Before I knew what I was doing, I was standing toe

to toe with him. He was a full foot taller than me, but that didn't stop me from glaring up at him with all the fire I could muster. With one hand on my hip, I used the other one to poke a finger against the center of his chest. Right between where I knew he had my and our mum's names inked on his skin.

"Don't you *dare* come at me like I'm some wayward underage teen caught smoking behind the school oval! I'm twenty-fucking-six years old, Donny! If I want to spend a night with a bloke, that's up to me. Not you."

His eyes had widened a moment when I used his birth name, but soon narrowed again before he grabbed my hand in his to stop me from poking him again.

"Dammit, Jacie. I knew I shouldn't have given in so easily when you refused to have one of the brothers shadow you at last night's party. You spent the whole night with this fool? Who was it? One of ours or a Satan's Cowboy? Who am I killing for daring to lay a finger on my sweet baby sister?"

Pulling my hand from his grip, I stepped back and rolled my eyes before glaring at him again.

"Oh, that's rich. I'm surprised lightning didn't strike you down just now. What a load of utter bullshit. Just because you're all about living the blissful married life now, dear brother, don't think for a moment that I haven't heard the bloody stories of how much of a man whore you were before Flick came along and *threw you on your arse.*"

I smirked at the blush that spread over his cheeks while he looked away as I'd finished speaking. Yeah, being called out wasn't fun. I was pretty damn sure Taz would prefer if no one remembered how, soon after he'd met Flick, he'd come up and grabbed her from behind at the club bar, Styx. Not realizing it was Taz, Flick had pulled some martial arts move that resulted in Taz being flat on his back in the middle of the bar. I would have paid big bucks to get a copy of that on video, but apparently no one was fast enough with their phone to record it. Damn shame that was.

"That's different!"

I cut him off, my temper flaring even brighter.

"Oh, don't you dare try to toss some bloody double standard garbage at me! I've been here eight months, Taz. *Eight fucking months.* I let your overbearing, overprotective bullshit slide in the beginning because I figured you couldn't help it while you adjusted to the knowledge that I was alive. But enough already! I'm a grown arse adult and can make my own choices. That includes if I want to have sex! We're not living in the Middle Ages where you get to control my life just because you've got a dick and I don't." I paused to shake my head. "And what the hell gives with you judging me for hooking up with a biker anyway? Since you're so happy living it up in the MC life, I'd have thought you'd be all over me being brought more fully into the fold."

He'd actually paled as I ranted, which left me speechless for a moment. Me having sex upset him that much? Damn. This being closer to my big brother thing was turning out to be a lot more complex than I'd anticipated.

After a minute or so, the loud shrill of Taz's phone snapped us both out of the awkward silence that had settled over us. Blowing out a breath, I ran my hands through my hair as I began to pace the room.

"Yeah, Mac?"

His eyes widened and he stumbled as he roared into the phone, "What the fuck do you mean she's bleeding?"

Instantly, everything else fell away, concern for my sister-in-law taking its place. Rushing to stand in front of my brother, I rested a palm on his shoulder, steadying him as I held his fear filled gaze with mine while he listened to whatever Mac was saying.

"I'll meet you at the hospital."

After he ended the call, he seemed to stall out. As though he couldn't quite process what was going on. Wrapping my arms around his waist I leaned in and gave him a tight hug for a few moments before releasing him to take charge.

"Let's get moving. I'll follow you. Unless you want to borrow one of the club cars and I'll drive you?"

Because Athena Security was a Charon MC owned business, and all the employees rode bikes, the club kept a couple of their cars here for when a case called for one to be used.

"Bikes will be faster. Let's go."

Quickly switching my sneakers for my riding boots, I grabbed my jacket, helmet and keys and was out the door, running to catch up to Taz who already had his dome on and was starting his bike.

Bridgewater was small enough of a town that it didn't take long to get anywhere, especially when you didn't care about speed limits or road rules. Following Taz, we got there in under five minutes and pulled into the parking lot at the same time Mac pulled up to the emergency entrance in his car.

Taz didn't bother turning off his bike before he dismounted and took off. When he paused a few meters away, taking his helmet off before he turned back, I called out to him.

"Leave your helmet there. I've got you covered. Go to Flick."

"Thanks, sis."

After setting it down, he sprinted to Mac's car, leaning into the front passenger seat to scoop his wife up into his arms before he turned and rushed inside with her. Once they were out of sight, I quickly got both our bikes sorted, with our helmets secured, before I hurried toward the entrance.

I hit the waiting room just as Taz was carrying Flick through to the back. I hoped Flick was being treated quickly because someone had called ahead, and not because she or the baby were in that much trouble. Knowing I wouldn't be allowed to go back with them, I went over to Mac.

"Did they say anything about what could be causing her to bleed?"

He moved his focus from the closed door to me, worry clear in his expression.

He shook his head. "Nah, they said nothing before they rushed her through. Guess I best go move the car. Be back in five."

I nodded and took a seat with a direct view of the door they'd gone through. Settling in to pray everything would be okay with Flick and the baby while I waited for news.

Chapter 8

Trident

As soon as we'd gotten back into Cutler last Sunday, Viper had sent a few of us right back out the door on a run over to Tyler. "Brothers first, brothers forever" is the SCMC's top rule. What the president wants, he gets is a close second. But his timing sucked. I had plans to spend the week tracking down my little runaway. I hadn't even gotten a chance to talk to Stone in all the rushing around. Once I was on my bike ready to ride out, but waiting on the others to get their shit sorted, I use the time to shoot off a text to him.

> Need you to give me Jacie's deets.
> Know you have them.

It was only moments before my phone buzzed with his reply.

> No can do, bro. Sorry. U need 2 get
> from her. Join me Fri night & I'll make it
> up 2U. Keep Sat free too.

What the fuck? He couldn't tell me? No doubt some sort of family loyalty bullshit I wasn't going to be able to talk my way around. Didn't mean I wasn't gonna try. And what in the hell was he on about wanting me to join him Friday night? Before I could text him back, the others came out, so I pocketed my phone, started my bike, and followed Tank's sled out of the clubhouse gates.

It was four long days later before I was finally back home and ready to track Stone down to get the answers the bastard had refused to give me all week. After parking my bike, I followed the others inside. Tank went straight for Viper's office to report in while the rest of us headed for the stairs.

Needing answers from Stone more than I needed to be clean, I decided to track the man down before I went and showered. As I made my way up to the first floor, I shot a text off to him.

Where U at?

The moment I passed through the doorway into the main room, Stone was hollering my way.

"Already told you, I ain't telling you shit, brother."

I stormed over to him.

"Why the fuck not? Brothers first remember?"

He nodded. "Yeah, but a woman's consent is just as fucking important and I won't break her trust, or Flick's."

Dammit, I couldn't argue with him on that one. While there were a few of the brothers who wouldn't have cared a lick if a woman consented to her details being shared around or not, Stone wasn't one of them. Normally, I wasn't either. I ran my hand through my beard, giving it a tug.

"Just come with me tonight, yeah?"

I shook my head with a smirk. "You're loving all this cryptic shit, aren't you? Where we going? Bridgewater?"

As much as I wanted to pin down my girl, I'd just ridden all day and didn't want to do another five hours tonight.

He grinned broadly. "Hell yeah, I am! Messing with you is the most fun I've had in a good long while. And I ain't telling you anything more than it's in Dallas and you don't need to wear anything special."

"Colors?"

He nodded. "Of course."

Realizing it was pointless to try to get anything more out of him, I headed toward the bar and grabbed a beer before I went and relaxed in a booth, dismissing the club girls that came over looking for some lovin'. There was only one woman I wanted in my lap, and she wasn't here.

Animal was high as a kite again, prowling after a club girl until he had her cornered. After a few minutes, Stone came and sat beside me with his own drink.

Being careful to keep my voice low, I turned my face toward Stone before I spoke. "We're gonna have to do something about him soon."

He nodded before taking a swig from his beer. "Yeah, I know. I keep hoping he'll pull himself outta this spiral he's in, but it's not looking like that's gonna happen."

I huffed out a breath at Stone's optimism. "How long has it been since you first noticed he was using too much?"

The other man stayed quiet for a few moments as we watched Animal roughly fuck the woman's mouth. Club whores knew the score. If they were here, they were to be available to any brother or other club guest, who wanted to use them. Any way they wanted. We didn't let them get hurt, if someone went too far, they paid a heavy price for it. But for the most part, it was only women who liked it rough who lasted any length of time here.

"I recon it didn't start to get outta control until about two, maybe three, months back."

I'd figured about the same timeline, but I wasn't as close to Animal as Stone was.

"You know what he's on?"

He shook his head. "I'm not certain. It ain't anything we move. I checked and he's never bought from the club. He ain't stupid enough to steal it. He knows the price for that."

Yeah. Death was the price. Suddenly I remembered something else.

"It was about what? Four months back that he fucked his shoulder up after dropping his bike?"

Stone closed his eyes and hit his head against the booth seat.

"Fuck. Yeah, he screwed his shoulder back in college and landing on it aggravated it. Dammit. He's probably gone and gotten himself hooked on whatever pills he was prescribed."

I gave my beard a tug. "If he ain't self-medicating from our stores, who the fuck is he buying from?"

Stone turned his glare on me. "You can't be thinking he's the reason we've been having issues with the cartel."

I shrugged. "Coincidences are rare. You know that better than fucking anyone. It might be time to talk to Maverick, or Viper."

Maverick was our VP and was a little more tolerant than Viper, our president. I didn't want to get the man taken out but he was going down a spiral that someone had to put a stop to before he ended up fucking killing himself, probably along with some others. Who would either be club brothers or innocents.

"Fuck!" Stone slammed a fist against the table, gaining us some attention from the others in the room for a few moments. Once they saw we weren't gonna start fighting, they all focused back on their own shit. Then on Animal when he snagged a second club girl who'd walked by him, tugging her over and spinning her around before he shoved her skirt up to give her ass several slaps as the first one continued to suck his cock. Then, pulling from the first one's mouth, he moved the second woman between them so he could thrust into her pussy from behind.

After a couple deep strokes, he reached around to wrap a hand in the first one's hair to pull her forward. She eagerly took the hint, licking at both his cock and the other girl's pussy.

Releasing her head, Animal tore open the second one's shirt, before he roughly gripped both her tits, using them to hold her down as he bucked into her hard. With a moan she wrapped her hands in her fellow club girl's hair, holding her in against her clit while Animal loosened his grip to tug on her nipples, twisting and pulling on them while he continued to fuck her hard.

As far as a live porn show went, it was pretty damn good. Especially when Tank went over to join them. Lifting the kneeling one's ass up till she was on all fours, he flipped up her skirt and tore her thong off. Undoing his jeans, he released his cock and shoved that monster in deep on a single thrust, shoving her face harder against the other chick's pussy.

I shifted in my seat as my cock throbbed, wanting some attention.

"Brother, you better not be pulling some stunt on me tonight. I will whoop your ass if you are because I need to be inside my woman before the sun sets, you feel me?"

Glancing over, I could see Stone's cheeks were flushed and he was moving around in his seat like he couldn't get comfortable while his gaze never left the show going on in front of us.

"Fuck, I need to let off some steam before we head out. I'll meet you out front at six."

It didn't escape my notice that once again the bastard had evaded answering my question and slipped out of the booth before I could call him on it. He made fast work of grabbing one of the other club girls, tossing her over his shoulder and heading down toward his room. Unlike Animal, Stone didn't like witnesses when he fucked. Another way me and Stone were similar.

Finishing off my beer, I headed back to my own room to get cleaned up and relieve some tension. I hoped like hell that Stone's cryptic shit meant I'd be seeing my little runaway tonight. No way would I risk her wrath by having her find out I fucked a club girl before going to her. It was already gonna be a battle to pin her down; I sure as fuck wouldn't risk it on some chick that meant nothing.

Chapter 9

Jacie

It was with a heavy heart that I left Bridgewater for Dallas. I'd offered to cancel the trip, to stay close to home to help Taz take care of Flick and Lolly, but Flick had refused to let me, demanding I still go. She'd told me that as much as she appreciated everything I'd been doing for them, she knew how much I'd been looking forward to the trip and I needed some time away to relax before returning and, no doubt, working my ass off again. Because now that Flick couldn't do housework or much of anything if she didn't want to risk going into early labor, she needed more help than ever.

Turned out Flick's bleeding was due to her having *placenta previa*. Which the doctor explained meant Flick's placenta was covering her cervix. I didn't know much about childbirth and pregnancy, but even I could work out that was some scary shit.

They'd kept her in hospital for forty-eight hours to monitor her and the baby. Thankfully, things down below were still solid, showing no signs of dilation, and she'd stopped bleeding by the time they released her. Her doctor had told her she was fine to go home, but she needed to rest as much as possible, no lifting or any other stresses.

The goal was to keep the baby inside her for as long as possible. But she was going to be spending a whole lot more time at the hospital over the next couple months for checkups and stuff than she'd originally planned. And she wouldn't be able to give birth naturally; she'd have to have a c-section for her and the baby's safety.

I would never forget the way my big brother had wobbled on his feet, nearly passing out when the doctor mentioned the high-risk Flick would be at of bleeding out if she went into labor naturally. I'd had to push aside my own shock and step up to steady him when he'd staggered, his face going as white as a ghost.

"Neveah? Crank the radio up. We need to get the vibes going on this road trip!"

Sparrow's sass had me smiling as Neveah, who was riding shotgun, grabbed her phone.

"I can do one better! I totally planned a playlist for the trip."

With a small shake of my head and a chuckle, I continued to focus on the highway. After eight months, I'd gotten mostly used to being on the other side of the road. But I still preferred to be the driver. Sitting in the front passenger seat, where I'd sat to drive in Australia, still messed with my head. Thankfully my crew didn't mind letting me drive.

While Neveah got her phone paired to the car's system Mirabelle leaned forward.

"What time is the dinner tonight again?"

I responded with a smile. "Six-thirty. We'll get there in plenty of time to clean up and change before then. No worries."

While, thanks to a whole lot of therapy, Mirabelle had come a long way since her rescue from a cult, she was still understandably nervous around strangers, especially men.

"Do you think there will be like real mobsters there? Or just models pretending."

Glancing in the mirror, I took in how she was chewing her lip and the concern in her gaze.

Sparrow reached over to grip her hand and give it a squeeze before she answered her. The club had freed Sparrow from a mob run brothel in L.A. a few years ago. She got Mirabelle in a way no one else could.

"Not honestly sure. I mean, I can't imagine a mobster with any sort of power lowering himself to being put on a cover of a romance novel. But if either of us recognize anyone in there from our pasts, we have our Plan B."

We all had panic buttons programed into our phones. We were to hit that sucker then wait for help to arrive. If they hadn't seen us, we were to keep it that way. If they had, we were to remain inside the main room, out in the open. Making sure to never be alone or allow them to get too close to us. Scout had told us he'd have back up there in minutes, which meant we had club shadows. I wasn't sure who Scout had sent, but would bet that Jazz was in the mix. None of us girls knew for sure what was between him and Sparrow since she'd never given us a straight answer whenever we'd asked, but only an idiot wouldn't notice the heat that flared between them whenever they got near each other. The hot glances they'd throw the other one's way at club barbecues were another giveaway.

"Right, time for fun! No more worrying."

Neveah started her playlist and turned it up. Taylor Swift's voice filled the car, telling us all to shake it off and we started singing along, the tension in the air fading away a little more with each new song that came on.

By the time we pulled up to the hotel in Dallas, I was in the zone for the weekend. We were rolling our bags into the lobby when Neveah grabbed my arm as she sucked in a breath.

"Is that Wander? Like for real. Damn, he's as pretty in real life as he is in photos. Not sure that's fair."

I glanced over and sure enough the sexy silver fox photographer, and model, was standing right there chatting with a woman who had awesome purple hair.

Sparrow came up on Neveah's other side. "And he's talking to Sapphire Knight. This is all so surreal."

I nodded. This was like some crazy dream. While I'd always read a lot, I'd never been to an event like this. Never met any of the authors I read, or seen any of the models in the flesh.

"C'mon, let's get checked in and cleaned up. Then we can come down and mingle."

We all headed over to the counter and queued up to wait our turn.

By the time we'd gone up to our adjoining rooms and settled in, it was time to get ready for the pre-event dinner. I was sharing with Neveah, while Mirabelle and Sparrow were in the other room. We had the adjoining door open and I sat back with a smile as the three of them chatted excitedly. I wanted to be as happy as they were, but I was worried. Taking out my phone I texted Flick.

Hey sis! Arrived safe. How U feeling?

I'd feel a lot better if I knew U were out having fun instead of worrying about me.

That had me smiling.

> Fine. I'll go have some fun if I have 2.
> But only because you're making me. So
> mean.

That earned me a heart emoticon that let me know I'd gotten her smiling at least.

Sparrow sat beside me on the bed. "All well back home?"

I nodded as I turned the screen off on my phone. "Yeah. I just feel bad for leaving. Like I'm needed back there, but I'm here at a book signing. It feels so unnecessary, frivolous now."

Sparrow wrapped her arms around my shoulders and rested her head against mine.

"Flick's well looked after, so is Taz and Lolly. You're not neglecting anyone by enjoying your birthday present. We all need to do things for ourselves sometimes. This trip might be for your birthday, but we're all here a little for ourselves too. You think it doesn't get tiring having Jazz up my butt twenty-four/seven?"

I chuckled and rolled my eyes. "Like you don't enjoy the attention."

Releasing me she huffed. "If he'd give me some damn attention I wouldn't mind, but no. He just stays back and watches. Like some creepy stalker."

Neveah joined us. "She bitching about Jazz again? We all know you *love* him. No point denying it."

Sparrow's face went red as she sputtered before speaking. "I do not! Not anymore at least. He's a pain in my ass who prevents me from having any fun. He's a killjoy. Not my heart's desire."

We all looked at her dumbfounded. She'd never said anything like this to us before. I had to wonder why she was suddenly so happy to chat about Jazz. With a hair toss, she lifted her chin defiantly, then focused her hazel eyes on me, giving me a slightly evil looking grin that left me feeling suddenly nervous.

"Plus, if rumors are to be believed, it was Jacie who got lucky last weekend. Not me. Who was it, girlfriend? No one is giving names! It's killing me!"

I shook my head. Realizing she'd only spoken about Jazz in the hopes that it would have me spilling my secrets in return.

"Oh, I'm not about to start to kiss-and-tell when you can't even admit to liking your guy. Now, let's get moving and go moon over some fake bikers who aren't creepy stalkers or a danger to our delicate selves."

"So there was a guy? Because you could have just snuck off by yourself to hide from Taz. Girls, we gotta get on this."

Shaking my head, I led the way to the door and out into the hallway with my giggling friends following me. Thankfully, by the time we'd reached the elevator, they'd quit hassling me and were chatting about books as we went down to the first floor where the dinner was being held.

"Do you think Kristine Allen will be here tonight? Or only tomorrow?"

I shrugged at Mirabelle's question. "No idea, babe. Guess we'll soon find out."

Entering the hotel restaurant, I scanned the room and quickly worked out where the MMM group was. Then I saw two men who had me nearly stumbling in shock.

"No fucking way. Not here. This was meant to be fake bikers, for fuck's sake! Not real ones!"

Sparrow frowned over toward where I was looking. "It's just a few of the Satan's Cowboys. They're friends to the Charons so it's all good. Looks like Stone and Trident. Oh and Animal. He's over there preening to some chicks."

Neveah gasped. "O.M.G! Which one is it? All three of them were at the fourth of July party; weren't they? Which one did you hook up with? Please tell me it wasn't Animal! He's just... no."

She mock shuddered in a way that had me chuckling despite my inner turmoil.

"It's not Animal."

Dammit. There was no way I was getting out of this without having to tell my girls about Trident. And I suspected that would be the least of my problems if he spotted me.

Chapter 10

Trident

"Where the fuck have you brought me?"

We'd come into downtown Dallas to some swanky hotel, parking next to Animal's bike near the entrance to their restaurant. He'd left the clubhouse a good ten minutes before us, and as far as I knew, didn't know we were trailing him, so it wasn't a surprise he wasn't outside waiting for us.

Looking inside, I could see exactly how many women were in there. Bit hard to miss, considering a bunch of them were now pressed up against the glass like we were gonna put on a show for them at any moment. At least with so many ladies in the one place, I had no doubts where Animal would be.

"Fuck, Trident. Wipe that look off your face before you scare off the women. It's a book event. Tomorrow is the main thing where they have a bunch of authors at tables selling their books and shit. Tonight's dinner is more of a casual catch up to chat thing."

I turned to glare at him. Was he for fucking real right now? "Seriously?"

He held his palms up in surrender, chuckling. "Hey, don't knock it til you've tried it, brother! This event? It's called MMM: Motorcycles, Mobsters and Mayhem. Trust me, these ladies read some pretty dark shit. And they do love a bad boy, especially a real live biker. Who am I to deny them?"

I really wasn't sure I liked this new version of Stone that laughed and joked like this. Prior to his sister finding him, he wouldn't have been caught dead anywhere near this place.

"How exactly do you know so much about all of this?"

Sick of feeling like a tiger in a zoo with so many folks staring my way, I left my bike and started toward the entrance. If Stone was forcing me to do this, I intended to get it done and over with as quickly as possible.

"Discovered it when I started watching over Animal a month or so ago. Got pulled in to join a shoot he was doing. It's not a bad gig. There's a heap of authors that write MC Romance and they want bikers on the covers. The more realistic, the better. And they're happy to fucking pay for the images."

I paused with one hand on the door.

"You're seriously telling me, there's books, like more than one, about bikers being romantic? And you and Animal are what? On the fucking covers? Man, you've both gone and lost your damn minds. It's embarrassing. For real."

Stone shoulder bumped me as he passed me and went inside ahead of me.

"Bastard. They're not making us out to be a bunch of Prince Charmings. Like I said, some of these ladies read some dark shit. Lots of suspense. Kink. Criminals. Vigilante justice. And it's fiction, for fuck's sake. Not like I'm giving away club secrets or anything." He shrugged a shoulder as we made our way toward the restaurant's entrance. "It was easy work and somethin' a bit different from the norm, and cash is always nice."

I huffed out a laugh as I shook my head. "Whatever, brother. You do you, man." As we entered the room, I scanned around, spotting Animal easily where he stood with his back to us, surrounded by women, young and old, fawning over him like he was some sort of rock star.

"You think he's high again? Is he gonna cause a scene?"

Stone winced as he rubbed a palm over the back of his neck. "Of course he's fucking high. Always is these days. He's definitely getting worse. But from what I've seen and heard, he's never caused any issues at shoots or events, so hopefully he'll keep his shit tight here. If not, well, that's the main reason I'm here, ain't it?"

"And me? I'm your backup for that? Because you better not have brought me here just so I can be mauled by a bunch of horny women. Or so you could trick me somehow into allowing some random snap photos of me."

He gave me a smirk that didn't reassure me in the least, and if a few ladies hadn't come over to chat with us at precisely that moment, I might have taken a swing at him for this stunt.

Asshole. He'd pay for this bullshit later, that was for sure.

"Well, hello there, ladies. How y'all doing this fine evening?"

Damn, Stone sure could turn on the charm when he wanted to. Allowing him to be the focus, I hung back, doing my best to look mean enough that no one would want to talk to me. It was working well and I was starting to relax when the hairs rose on the back of my neck. Instantly on full alert, I scanned the room, searching carefully for any threats I might have missed earlier.

When I spotted her standing with a couple of other Charon MC ladies, I cursed under my breath.

My runaway had come to SCMC territory. Fucking perfect.

Stone grabbed my shoulder and leaned in to whisper near my ear.

"Told you to trust me, brother."

Not wanting to lose her in the crowd, I only glanced at Stone for half a second. "You knew she'd be here?"

"Yeah, it was her birthday last weekend. This is her celebration. Girls' weekend away. Although, she nearly didn't make it when Flick ended up in hospital."

I frowned but didn't take my gaze off my woman. "What do you mean? What the fuck happened?"

"Flick started bleeding. She and the baby should both be fine; so long as she takes it real easy and rests a lot for the remainder of her pregnancy. Jacie's been doing a lot around the house for them. She's a good one, Trident. You pin her down, you better not fuck it up. A lot of folks will be after you if you do."

I gritted my teeth for a moment before I said something I shouldn't in public. We were both speaking quietly, but it wouldn't take much for those around us to hear what we were saying if shit got heated.

"Ain't fucking telling you again, Stone. She's already mine, and I'd never fucking hurt her."

Before he could say another word, I strode away from him and toward my girl. Brushing off the few ladies who tried to snag my attention, I didn't stop until I was standing in front of Jacie and her friends.

"Well, fancy seeing you here, my little runaway. You didn't tell me it was your birthday last weekend. Would have gotten you a present had I known."

One of the girls, I was pretty sure her name was Sparrow, let out a whoop.

"*Dayumn*, girl! You've been holding out on us!"

I glared her way as she started fanning herself with her hand.

"What the fuck are you on about?"

Muttering under her breath something about friends and enemies, Jacie grabbed my wrist and pulled me away from them.

"Don't worry about Sparrow. She's just trying to rile me up."

The daggers Jacie sent the girl's way, along with how Sparrow had raised a brow while she grinned broadly at us proved she had done more than just try. Since Jacie was leading me where I wanted to go, toward the exit of the restaurant and away from the crowd, I wasn't gonna say that out loud and risk her stopping.

Once we got into the lobby, she stalled out. Clearly she hadn't planned further than escaping her friends. Twisting my wrist free of her hold, I rested my palm on her lower back and guided her toward the main doors. When we were out in the warm evening air, I kept us moving around the side of the hotel away from all the glass windows and into a garden area. Scanning around, I found a corner that would have us hidden from most people who might pass by. Thankfully, since it was early evening, when most folks had dinner, there weren't many people around.

Backing her up against the wall, a large tree to her side, I boxed her in. One palm on the concrete beside her head while I rested the other one loosely around the base of her throat.

Wrapping one of her hands around my wrist at her

neck, she pressed the other against my chest, trying to push me away. When I didn't budge, she glared at me.

"Getting déjà vu here, T."

Damn, her sass got to me. I couldn't help but tease her in return.

"That right, girlie?"

Her chin went up and fire lit her eyes. "Told you before, I ain't no girl."

Growling, I grew serious. Without releasing her, I moved my hand, tightening my grip up higher on her neck so I could keep her face tilted up toward me.

"And I told you, that you were mine. I fucking *claimed* you, Jacie. You *accepted* that claim then fucking snuck out on me and *hid*. You fucking hid like a scared child."

The muscles of her jaw tightened as she ground her teeth, and fire continued to light her gaze. I had no fucking clue why this woman and her sassy bitchiness drew me in like it did. But I couldn't deny that I was completely hooked on her.

"Maybe you need a reminder of what you'll lose if you keep running off."

Slamming my lips over hers, I devoured her mouth, thrusting my tongue in when she moaned. I continued to kiss her as I moved my body in closer, until I was pressed tight against her, my leg between hers. With a shudder, she dug her nails into my shoulders and ground down on my thigh.

Chapter 11

Jacie

Bloody hell, this man could kiss. By the time he pulled back, I was breathless, panting to catch my breath, and my body was on fire. Lava flowed through my veins and if it wasn't for the sounds of downtown Dallas cutting through my fog of arousal, I might have begged him to fuck me right here, right now.

Resting a forearm against the wall above my head, he held my gaze while he stroked my face with his free hand. The calluses on his fingertips sensitized my skin until I was trembling, desperate for more of him.

"Trident..."

My voice was more moan than anything, but it was all I could manage with how he'd scrambled my brain.

"You got a room here we can go to, *Ula'ula Mõ'ī?*"

There was that weird name he called me again.

"What does that mean? *Ula'ula Mõ'ī.*"

"It's a Hawaiian endearment. Room?"

That didn't really tell me what it meant, but he clearly wasn't going to give me any more of an explanation right now.

"Yeah, I'm staying here but I'm sharing with

Neveah. We'll have the room to ourselves until dinner finishes up."

After giving me a quick, hard kiss, he straightened.

"I'll take what I can get. Let's go."

Even though it was a warm evening, a chill washed over me once he was no longer pressed up against me. I was rubbing at the goose bumps on my arms when Trident reached out and took my hand in his, tangling our fingers together before pulling me toward the hotel entrance. Keeping my eyes forward, I was careful to match my steps to Trident's, so I stayed mostly hidden by his much larger body as we passed through the lobby.

By some sort of miracle, the moment we entered the alcove that housed the bank of elevators, one opened. After those inside exited, we followed another couple in and I tapped the button for the fourth floor as I passed the controls. Trident then pulled me in against him, moving me until my back was to his front before he wrapped his arms around my waist. Ignoring the looks the other couple gave us, I leaned my head against his shoulder, closing my eyes with a smile when he dropped a soft kiss on my temple. I couldn't believe how all his possessive bullshit was actually doing it for me. I'd have knocked another man on his arse if they'd pulled even half of what Trident had. But instead of telling him to knock it off and standing apart from him to prove to the world how independent I was, here I was, snuggling into him. Closing my eyes to fully enjoy how safe and cherished I felt in his embrace.

It really was complete and utter craziness.

When the doors opened on my floor, Trident's palm returned to rest on my lower back as I led the way down the hall toward my room. The sweetness we'd shared in the elevator had soothed the frenzied energy that had ruled us earlier, so by the time we entered the hotel room my mind had cleared enough I could think of more than ripping his clothes off.

Leaving Trident to handle the main door, I moved to the one that joined this room to Sparrow and Mirabelle's, closing and locking it. Once that was done, I leaned against the wall beside it, smiling at Trident doing his thing. He'd finished securing the door and was now reconning the area. Poking his head into the bathroom before scanning the rest of the very nondescript room.

"Safe enough for you?"

With a glare my way, he finished checking the window before striding toward me until he stood toe-to-toe with me. Crossing his arms across his chest, he stared into my eyes.

"I will always make sure you are safe, Jacie. *Always.* Now; tell me. Why'd you ghost me last weekend?"

Heat crept up my neck and over my face and I bit the inside of my cheek, not wanting to answer him. But I knew he wasn't going to let me get away with silence.

"You ashamed to have been with me? Embarrassed?"

That had my jaw dropping and shock pinging through my brain. Was he nuts? "What? Of course not! Why would you even think that?"

He shrugged a shoulder with feigned casualness. I'd really hurt him with how I'd snuck away. Guilt tore up my gut at the damage I'd done by being such a wuss.

"Well, let's see. I'm a lot older than you, for a start. Then there's the fact I'm from a one percenter club. We play harder than the Charons ever will."

I shook my head, before running my fingers through my hair, pushing the curls back behind my ears.

"I can't believe you—"

His palms slamming against the wall on either side of my head had my mouth closing mid-sentence.

"Yeah, well, I can't believe you'd be such a little coward either. But you fucking were. Sneaking off on me the first chance you got." He tilted his head. "Unless I really read you wrong, and you pull this stunt on the regular. Or maybe I was just a happy little birthday present, nothing more. I can think of several different reasons of why you did what you did, babe. But I'd like to hear the motherfucking truth from your lips. So tell me, Jacie Lewis, why'd you run from me last weekend?"

Frustration coursed through me, mixed with anger because dammit, he had a point. Shame also weighed me down. I wasn't proud of what I'd done, especially now that he was standing close enough I could smell the leather of his cut, while he called me out.

"I assumed you'd just gotten caught up in the moment. You know? Like in the movies when a guy gets horny and promises a girl the world only to be done with her by morning. Figured I'd avoid that scene, save us both the trouble and get out first." I paused, looking down at my feet before continuing, "Not too many people have ever stuck by me. I, ah, try to avoid adding new rejections into my life if I can."

Moving his hand, he curled a finger under my chin and gently forced my face up.

"Look at me, *Ula'ula Mõ'ī.*"

With a wince, I slowly lifted my gaze to his. My breath caught at the gentleness in his dark irises.

"First up, your momma didn't choose to leave you, yeah? Neither did your brother. From what I've heard about Taz, if he'd known you were alive, he would have moved heaven and earth to keep you safe and by his side. Secondly, you get that in your desperation to avoid feeling pain, you just transferred it to me, yeah?"

My throat clogged with emotion while tears stung my eyes. As much as I'd always respected people who were straight shooters, I didn't appreciate being forced to examine myself so deeply. "I'm sorry. I never meant to—"

He cut me off again, this time with a shake of his head.

"It's done, babe. Over. But we ain't doing this again. Me and you are gonna be fucking open and honest with each other from here on out, you feel me? No matter how much you think I don't wanna hear it, know that I do."

I frowned. "Not sure that's exactly realistic, T. I work for a security firm, and you're in a MC. We're both gonna have secrets we can't share."

He tapped his forefinger against my nose before straightening and folding his arms over his chest like he'd done earlier.

"So much sass. Yeah, babe. We won't be sharing shit that's not ours to share, but anything that affects us? That, we tell each other. I won't have bullshit coming between us."

With a raised eyebrow, I mirrored his pose, arms crossed over my breasts.

"Why do you even care so damn much? I mean, we just met last weekend, and only had one night together. Which, in case you don't remember, started with us fighting. Now you're saying I've insulted and hurt you. How can you even want to see me?"

He chuckled, the low gravely sound lighting me up, hardening my nipples that thankfully where hidden behind my forearms.

"Now that I know you didn't sneak off to be cruel, just to protect yourself—that's easy to forgive, *Ula'ula Mō'i*. And we weren't fightin' last weekend. That was just a little verbal sparring to get the blood pumping. Just so happens I like your fire, Jacie. Like it a fuck of a lot. So much so, I've spent way too much of my time this week fantasizing about all the ways I could put that smart mouth of yours to use when I caught up with you."

Groaning, I looked to the ceiling and tapped my head against the wall.

"Why must all the pretty ones be such alpha-holes?"

His low growl had a shiver running up my spine. Instinct had me side stepping away from him before turning to dash across the room. A heartbeat later, I was face down on the bed, sandwiched between his large, hot body and the mattress, my wrists once again in one of his hands, but this time they were trapped against my lower back. I tried to buck him off, to wriggle free, but couldn't move him. With a low growl, he leaned in and nipped at the edge of my ear.

"I'm not sure what to be more insulted over: you calling me pretty, or whatever the fuck an alpha-hole is."

Twisting my head to the side and blowing my hair out of my face, I glared daggers at him.

"Take your pick, babe. Because while you might be nice to look at, whenever you open your damn mouth, your inner alpha-male-arsehole comes out, destroying the illusion of you being any sort of Prince Charming."

His grin was wicked as he tilted his head down, one sexy eyebrow going up.

"Really? You trying to tell me you don't like me just as I am? That you don't get hot and wet for me? Because remember that little rule I just made about lying? I didn't expect you to go breaking it so fucking fast, *Ula'ula Mō'ī*. Prince Charming is always such a sissy. I'm more like a knight in shining armor—make that a knight on a shining Harley. I'll come to your rescue any day..."

He ground his erection in against my butt. I tugged at my hands, anger mixing with the arousal I wasn't going to admit to. "Release me, dammit!"

"Ask nice, and I'll think about it."

Swallowing down a growl, I took a deep breath before I cleared my throat, putting on my sweetest tone.

"Trident, could you *please* let me go."

He stilled, like I'd shocked him. Then with a bark of laughter he rose up off me, but before I could celebrate my freedom, he was lifting me, turning me over and moving me further up the bed, so my head was now on the pillow. Then he settled in beside me while I lay there trying to catch my breath.

"I'm not a damn doll, T!"

I wanted to hate the way he could move me around how he pleased with such ease, but there was no denying the liquid heat that just soaked my knickers.

Leaning his head down he nipped at my chin before hovering his lips over mine.

"You are to me, *Ula'ula Mō'ī*." And, Jacie, I ain't ever letting you go, you're fucking mine. You agreed to that last weekend. And considering I can fucking smell how wet you are for me right now, you're still on board with that plan."

I opened my mouth to say something. I wasn't sure what. My mind and body were at war. I didn't want a biker, not for the long haul. Sure, I'd been wanting to hook up with one for my birthday last weekend. But that hadn't been me looking for Mr. Right, more like Mr. Right Now. All the possessive ownership bullshit bikers pulled was not my jam. It was way too close to the mobster garbage my dad had tried to pull with Mum whenever Donny wasn't around.

In the end it didn't matter that I couldn't find the words because Trident lowered his lips to mine, and all thoughts other than "more" left my head. He swiped his tongue into my open mouth and I eagerly tangled mine with his, moaning as he took control of our kiss, mastering me with his mouth. Reaching my palms up, I cupped either side of his face, keeping him close and the kiss going.

Chapter 12

Trident

Fuck, this woman owned me heart and soul. Thankfully she didn't seem to know it. I had a feeling the moment she did, she'd never let me forget it.

Breaking off our kiss, I stayed close enough our breaths mingled, keeping my gaze on hers.

"Say it, Jacie. Tell me you're fucking mine. No one else's."

The arousal that darkened her pretty blue irises began to clear as she frowned.

"Why?" She cleared her throat. "Why are you so determined to claim me? We haven't known each other long enough for you to be this possessive."

Moving back, I returned to lie on my side beside her. We were both breathing heavily from our make out session and my gaze went to the rise and fall of her chest. As I pondered how to answer her, I reached out and started fiddling with the chunky gold-plated sun pendant she wore on a matching chain. It didn't seem like something Jacie would pick for herself. She certainly hadn't been wearing it last weekend.

Blowing out a breath, I started talking, trying to get her to understand.

"I learned young to always trust my instincts. Then, on my first deployment in the Marines, I'd been too worried about what my team would think of me to tell anyone how my instincts were screaming, and it didn't end well. So now I do. Good or bad. Last weekend? I wasn't expecting to actually like you. Initially I followed you inside simply to keep you safe. But from the moment I got my first good look at you, heard you turn that bratty mouth of yours on me, I just knew. You were meant for me. I'm old enough to not want to waste time pussy-footing around when I find a good thing."

"What do you mean you intended on keeping me safe? I was in my brother's clubhouse. Not sure how I could have been much safer."

Scoffing at her comment, I kept looking at that sun of hers.

"Safe. Yeah. Not sure you know what happened with Taz and Flick a few years back?"

I caught her nod in my peripheral vision. "Probably know more than you about that one. But basically, Flick's uncle owned property in Bridgewater your club wanted. Not realizing Flick was an old lady, some of your men came and snatched her. Stone recognized her as his sister, busted her out of a cell. She busted a bunch of SCMC asses before they were both tossed back in a cell and Taz and the Charons rode up to reclaim her."

I wondered what the fuck she could know that I didn't about that situation, but now wasn't the time to get into it.

"Animal, Tank and a couple other younger guys were the ones Flick took down. They've not exactly forgiven her for it. But she's a pregnant old lady so: untouchable. You, on the other hand, my independent fiery woman, are unpatched and unprotected by club law."

She sat up with a gasp and turned to face me.

"I'm Taz's sister, a blood relative of the Charon MC. I *am* protected."

Sighing, because I knew this wasn't going to make her happy. I shifted until I was sitting with my back against the headboard before I reached for her, scooping her up and putting her sideways over my lap, so I could keep my arm around her waist to stop her from running.

"The Charons would see it that way, but Animal has made it clear he doesn't. Thinks it means that he won't suffer any repercussions for going after you. Animal isn't in a good place. Fuck. I shouldn't be telling you this, but I'm thinking it best you know what you're walking into with him. He's using. We're not one hundred percent sure, but we think he got himself hooked on pain pills after he re-injured his shoulder a couple months back."

She was nearly vibrating with rage as I tightened my hold on her.

"Are you trying to tell me you only claimed me to keep me safe from your club brother? Who's fucked up on drugs, but apparently you guys won't do anything about it other than watch him spiral? Seriously? That's what you're saying to me?

Closing my eyes for a moment, I huffed out a breath. Me and my stupid no lying rule. Should have waited until after this conversation to put that sucker in place. Fuck!

"It's not that simple. We rat him out to the club president and it's not what we suspect, we could be signing his death warrant for no fucking reason. For now, a few of us are watching him closely, trying to work out exactly what's going on. If it is just pain pills, we'll sort something out. Probably a snatch and grab, knock him out and shove him into one of the cells at the clubhouse until he dries the fuck out. Maybe toss his butt into rehab. But we need more facts before we go getting Viper involved. He's got enough on his plate without adding this." Although, I was pretty sure he already knew something was going on. It wasn't like Animal had been careful with who saw him behaving like a fucking lunatic. "And as far as claiming you? That has fuck all to do with Animal. If I'd just wanted to keep you safe from the others, I would have just stayed near you last weekend. Could have told Taz and he would have taken you with him when he took Flick home. I claimed you because you were fucking made to be mine, Jacie. Only mine."

Wrapping my fingers around her jaw, I moved her face so I could get my mouth on her again. Kissing her seemed to be one of the few things that could disarm her temper. Which was damn convenient because I just so happened to fucking love getting my mouth on my woman.

Ending the kiss, I rested my forehead against hers so I could take her scent deep into my lungs. Playing with the sun pendant she was wearing again, I gave it a light tug to get her focusing on it. "Why do you wear this?"

Her whole body stiffened, and disappointment that she still didn't trust me enough to share her secrets was a sour taste in the back of my throat as I dropped the necklace back down against her skin.

"Nevermind. Forget I asked."

I hadn't changed my mind. This woman was my ride or die, I *knew* it deep in my soul. I just wished she felt the same way already, but she needed more time, I got that. She didn't trust her instincts like I did mine. But fuck, I was impatient for when she would put her faith in me.

"It's the only thing I have left of my mum." She

looked down, picking the charm up herself. "When I was little, I'd cling to this thing. Whenever I got really upset, she'd take it off and let me wear it, or hold it until I felt better. The day she died—was murdered—her and Gordon had been arguing. I can't remember what it was about, just that there was a whole lot of yelling. I wasn't quite three years old." She huffed a half laugh. "Probably too young to be left alone with this thing. Choking hazard, right? But I never even once tried to put it in my mouth that I recall. Mum had been crying when she'd wrapped the chain around my neck, told me she loved me more than the sun loved the moon, then closed my door. I hated when she was upset like that. Hated Gordon and his bullshit. His friends in their stuffy suits that'd come over." She shook her head. "I must have cried myself to sleep before the smoke got into my lungs. Donny pulled me out when he got home from school..."

She stalled out and I pressed a kiss to her temple, my heart breaking for that little toddler who lost so much that day.

"I'm glad you have it."

She nodded and sniffled, before she blew out a breath. "Damn, that dampened the mood a bit, huh?"

Lifting her hand to my mouth I pressed a kiss to the center of her palm before I placed it under my cut, over my heart.

"Rest for a bit, babe. We got all the time in the world."

For what had to be the first time since I met her, she didn't argue, just snuggled into my chest and dozed off. It wasn't long before I shuffled us down the bed, keeping her on top of me, before nodding off myself.

Chapter 13

Trident

When I stirred awake about twenty minutes later, it was to find my arms still full of a sleeping woman. The fact she hadn't tried to sneak off on me, that she'd shared something so personal, made herself vulnerable to me before we'd fallen asleep, gave me hope I was getting somewhere with her. With a quiet sigh, she squirmed against me and my cock—which was already rock hard—began to throb with need.

Rolling us over, caging her beneath me, I kissed my way along her jawline until I was close to her ear.

"Time to wake up, *Ula'ula Mō'ī.*"

Reaching up, she wrapped an arm around my neck, pulling me in as she rolled us to the side.

"Not yet. It's not." Her voice was adorably slurred.

Trying not to laugh, I pulled her hand from my neck and pressed a kiss to the center of her palm, like I had earlier, before nipping each of her fingertips.

"C'mon, babe. Got plans I need you awake for."

She pulled her hand out of my grip and tucked it under her cheek.

"Hmm, but wanna sleep, T."

Chuckling at how stubborn my girl was, I grabbed

her hip and turned her toward me so I could give her jean clad butt a playful smack. With a squeal she rolled back onto her side to glare at me as she gave my chest a shove with a fist.

"What the fuck, Trident? Did you seriously just *spank* me?"

I tapped her nose with my forefinger.

"Damn straight I did. And I'll do it again if you don't start doing what you're told. You left me hanging last weekend. Woke up with morning wood and no one to take care of it. I ain't having that happen again. And since I got no clue how long your girls are gonna give us, I'm done wasting time."

She stilled, mouth open as she blinked at me for a few seconds before her gaze narrowed and my heart rate ticked up. Fucking loved riling my woman up. She was hotter than hell when she got going.

"I left you hanging... You know you can take care of your dick all by yourself, yeah? Not my fault you didn't rub one out before you took off home."

The mouth on this chick.

"Trust me, I tried that. Turns out after my cock got a taste of you, my palm just wasn't gonna cut it. So, you gonna strip yourself or do I need to do it for you? Although, I can't guarantee your clothes will survive if I do it."

She sputtered and cursed before she rolled over and stood beside the bed and pointed back at me.

"You're an arse! Telling me to strip after spanking my butt does not count as foreplay. For fuck's sake." She shook her head, anger putting fire in her gaze that shouldn't turn me on more, but it so fucking did. "I'm done with this bullshit. And with you. Go find some other chick to stalk. I'm going back down to my friends."

Oh hell no was she leaving. Not this room and not me. No fucking way.

Springing up from the bed I rushed over and caught her before she could get more than a few steps. Slinging her over my shoulder, I returned to the bed and tossed her onto the mattress. With a squeal of outrage, she shoved her hair out of her face. I started speaking before she could.

"We had this trouble last weekend too. Seems you have a real issue when it comes to following directions. That ain't gonna fly, babe. Don't mind if you're doin' it to fire me up, but I get the feeling you're playing some sort of alpha game that you ain't gonna win, babe. And if you try to pull this in front of the brothers, that little tap I gave you earlier is nothing on what I'll be forced to do. Club rules, Jacie. Disrespect ain't taken lightly. And punishment would be public."

In the bedroom, if she wanted to play that way every now and then, that was more than fine with me. I'd always push back, prove to her I was strong enough to be everything she needed her man to be. Then I'd have her screaming in pleasure until she forgot about anything else but the orgasms I could give her. But I wasn't gonna tolerate her refusing to do every single fucking thing I asked of her. Especially not when we weren't alone.

She shook her head, and I swear her eyes glossed over with tears for just a moment, along with a flash of fear and vulnerability, before her lips pressed into a firm line and the fire of her temper took over, pushing all her other emotions aside.

After sitting up, she moved to kneel, then shuffled over until she was close enough she could shove at my chest with both her palms. Anticipating she'd do just that, I'd braced myself so I barely moved which just ignited her fury all the more.

"If that's what you need, then why the fuck do you want me? Clearly, I'm not nearly submissive enough for you. And I won't change. I will never be some little 'yes' woman. Why don't you just cut bait and run, yeah? Find some chick who's happy to let you mold her into whatever the fuck you want her to be."

Running a hand over my beard, I gave it a tug. Taking a minute to think before I responded to her. That earlier flash of emotions, before her rage took over, had shocked me. These games she was playing were more serious than I first thought they were. She'd mentioned earlier how not many people stuck by her. But I thought we'd dealt with that. Was she really so scared of being rejected, of her having her heart broken, that she'd push me away rather than giving us a chance to be more? While we hadn't exactly talked kids and white picket fences, I'd figured she was the type to want those things. Especially given the way she adored her niece.

I wanted to growl in frustration. Because I couldn't make sense of what was running through her head, I wasn't sure what to do to fix it. Also knew from the stubborn angle of her jaw, she wasn't currently in the mood to delve into her psyche. The only way forward I could see was to just keep reassuring her.

"Don't get me wrong, Jacie. I don't mind being challenged, or playing games when we're in private. Fucking love that you're brave enough to hold your ground with me, not afraid to show me how strong that spine of yours is. Having a little yes woman who'd never fucking protest anything I said or did holds zero appeal. A strong, fiery woman who is perfectly capable and happy to be Miss Independent, but *chooses* to stand beside me and let me support her? Who is not afraid to call me on my shit? Now *that* holds a fuck of a lot of appeal. All I need from you right now is for you to tell me you'll be mine, exclusively mine, and we can move this on to the part we've both been looking forward to."

She shook her head, frowning, confusion clouding her eyes. Did she honestly not understand how much of a fucking treasure she was? How any man with more than half a brain would want her for his old lady? The mother of his kids. Would be willing to kill or die to keep her safe.

With her hands on her hips, she looked down and rolled her lips in, obviously thinking her answer through. Nerves had me wanting to twitch, but I held the sensation off. Who knew all those years with the USMC would help me hold strong in the face of my woman?

After taking a deep inhale she lifted her gaze to mine and licked her lips. Clenching my jaw, I held my damn breath as I waited for her answer. I honestly didn't know what she was gonna say. She was just as likely to tell me to fuck off as she was to say she was mine. Maybe I shouldn't have put it all on the line this soon, but I wasn't about to keep pussy-footing around her with this shit. I knew what I wanted: her. And I was getting too old for the bullshit games where we chased each other's tails for years before settling down. Fuck that shit. I wanted her committed to me now.

"Fine. I'm yours. Exclusively." I grinned and she held a finger up. "For now. I ain't wearing a ring yet. And that also means you're completely mine. I am *not* the type of woman to accept her man screwing around on her. I know all about MCs and their club whores. You touch one of them and you better be prepared to wake up missing body parts I'm sure you'd rather keep attached, you understand me?"

Fuck me, even the way she accepted my claim with a threat did something for me. She was truly my *Ula'ula Mõ'ī*, my red queen.

With a broad grin, I reached for her, gripping her hips and tugged her forward. She wrapped her arms around my neck as she pressed her body up against mine, lifting her face to me. I took the invitation and slammed my mouth down over hers. Devouring her mouth, claiming her, as I slid my hands up her back, under her shirt to flick open her bra. Moving her hands, she scraped her nails along either side of my head, through the hair I kept buzzed short. The tremor it caused to flow through me had me ending the kiss and closing my eyes on a moan.

"Fuck, that feels good, *Ula'ula Mõ'ī*."

Shoving up to her feet, Jacie threw herself at me, her legs going around my waist and her hands clutching my shoulders. Not expecting the move, I stumbled back a step before I caught my balance, instinctively wrapping my arms around her to hold her to me as I did.

"Whoa!"

Burying her face in my neck, she kissed and nibbled at my skin while she ground her pussy against my cock.

"Fuck, babe. Love how hot you get for me." I'd have liked it a whole lot more if we were naked. Damn clothes getting in the way. "Gonna need you to start wearing skirts. If you were wearing one right now, all I'd need to do is unzip and tear your panties away to be deep inside you, where I know you want me."

With a groan, she swirled her tongue in a small circle on my neck, before sucking on the same spot, no doubt leaving a mark in her wake. I had to chuckle at my fiery woman staking her claim, marking me where everyone would see it, as I had done to her last weekend. My brothers would give me hell for it, but I couldn't get mad at her. Not when I fucking loved that she was feeling as possessive as I was. Not that she ever needed to worry about me stepping out on her. I'd never been one to fuck around when I had a woman, and I certainly had no intention of starting now that I'd found my One. My ride or die.

Returning to stand by the bed, I leaned down until her back was against the mattress. After kissing her again, I pulled her hands from around my neck and straightened.

Neither of us needed to say a word to know what we both were thinking. Desire shone bright in her gaze, and I was sure she was seeing the same damn thing in mine. Shrugging out of my cut, I moved to hang it over the back of the chair, then emptied my pockets onto the seat before I turned back to Jacie, and stalled out at what I saw.

She was sitting on the edge of the mattress and, having stripped out of her shirt, she slid her bra free and tossed it on the floor. Then she paused, looking my way with a raised brow.

"See something you like, T?"

"I see my woman looking sexy as fuck."

Reaching over my head, I grabbed a fist full of my t-shirt and tugged it off before I tossed it toward the chair. After toeing off my boots, and peeling off my socks, I turned back to my woman, who was now standing next to the bed facing me, her low lidded gaze locked on my bared chest as she chewed on her lower lip.

"Looks like you're enjoying the view just as much, *Ula'ula Mō'ī*."

Fuck she was a sight. She'd followed my lead, and was now barefoot, her bright blue painted toenails a striking contrast to her pale skin and the cream carpet. She stood proud, her shoulders back so those sweet tits of hers were thrust toward me, her nipples already hard. I stroked my beard, giving it a tug as I remembered how good she tasted, how I could make her call out my name by just suckling on those dusky pink tips.

She spoke on a sigh. "So damn pretty."

With a grin, I raised an eyebrow at her.

"Pretty? Seriously, babe?"

With a dreamy look in her eyes, she nodded.

As much as I wished she'd used a less feminine word to describe me, I wasn't gonna complain about how she clearly liked my body. Made all the hours I put in to maintaining it worthwhile. Well, the fact I could still take care of business, handing a man his ass with ease to keep myself and my club protected was the main reason I trained, but the way my woman zoned out from just looking at my muscles was a damn nice bonus.

Ignoring my throbbing dick for the moment, I sauntered over to her, undoing my belt and pulling it from my jeans as I did. After tossing it toward her pile of clothes, I cupped her face between my hands and kissed her. Her palms rested against my pecs as she leaned into me. When her mouth opened, I slipped my tongue in to dance with hers, moaning as her sweet taste filled my mouth. She already had me hooked, totally addicted to her. I would always crave this woman, never tire of her. In just one week, she'd become as important as the air I breathed. It was insane, but true.

Moving my hands down to cup her ass, I kneaded her rounded globes through her jeans, wishing we were both naked as I pulled her in until my erection was pressing against her stomach. She dug her fingers into my chest before she smiled, breaking our kiss. Opening my eyes, I cocked a brow at the sparkle in her gaze, but before I could say a word, my sassy woman tweaked both my nipples.

I growled as lightning jolted through me, landing in my cock which throbbed and jerked with need. With a small moan, her eyes bright with lust, she squirmed against my aching dick.

"Need to be inside you, Ula'ula Mō'ī."

She rose up on her toes and pressed a kiss to the corner of my mouth.

"Soon, babe."

Then she kissed a path from my shoulder, over my pecs. As she moved down, my hands slipped from her ass up her back. Stroking her soft skin, playing with the ends of her hair. When she sucked, then nipped at each of my nipples, my whole body stilled as another shot of lightning fired through me.

My brain short-circuited, torn between tossing her on the bed and tearing her pants off so I could fuck her, and letting her continue, hoping she'd keep going lower. I was a live wire, panting for breath, when she started licking over the dips and rises of my abs. Then the sassy woman slipped her fingers inside my waistband, stroking over the tender skin of my lower stomach before bumping into my cockhead through my underwear.

"Woman, have mercy."

With her blue irises bright with delight she looked up at me. That big grin on her face as she continued to run a finger around the tip of my dick almost made this teasing torture she was putting me through worth it.

"You wanna taste of me, babe?"

Her gaze darkened with arousal, and I caught a flash of her white teeth as she bit at her lower lip. Gripping her chin, I used my thumb to pull the flesh free.

"You're gonna hurt yourself if you keep that up. No

pressure, babe. But fuck, I'd love to know how your mouth feels on my cock. You've got me so fucking hard, I won't last long."

"I've never..." She pulled from my grip, lowering her gaze as her cheeks reddened.

Fuck, she was just too damn precious. I dropped to my knees in front of her, cupping her face to guide her to look at me.

"You saying you've never had a man's dick in your mouth or that you've never had one cum down your throat?"

That blush of hers grew darker. She licked her lips before she answered me.

"The second one. Although, I'm not exactly an expert at the first one either."

Fuck, she slayed me. So fucking innocent for a woman so damn feisty. I leaned in and kissed her, starting out gentle before deepening things as I grew hungrier for her. Dropping my hands from her face, I cupped her breasts. Kneading the mounds before tweaking her nipples, tugging and twisting them until she was moaning and pawing at me.

Ending the kiss, I rose back to stand, undoing my fly as I did. Shoving my jeans and underwear down my legs in one move, I kicked them free, loving how my woman's gaze was glued to my hard length. Licking her lips, she reached a hand toward me, running a fingertip from the head down to my balls. Clenching my jaw, I tried to push down my rising arousal. I wanted to give her all the time she needed to explore and learn me, but fuck, I was so damn horny, I wasn't sure how long I'd be able to give her.

When she pressed one palm to my thigh and wrapped the other one around my length before giving me a tentative stroke, I wondered if she'd been bullshitting me about not being an expert. Because damn, while I've had a lot of women blow me over the years, I'd never been this close to the edge from just a woman's hand on my dick. Closing my eyes for a minute, I thought unsexy thoughts. Football. A bunch of us had gone to see the Texans take on the Chiefs. Only for them to fucking lose. Chiefs won with a lead of twenty points, making for a shitty night because a few of the brothers had put money down and were mad at having lost it.

I blew out a breath, glad to have found a way to pull back from coming so soon. Focusing back on my woman, I wrapped my hand over hers, guided her on how to stroke me, how tight I liked to be gripped, before I released her to let her keep going on her own.

"Use your other hand to cup my balls, baby."

Spreading my legs for her, she slipped her other hand between my thighs. When she cupped my balls in her palm, my whole body jolted at the timid contact that had me right back where I'd been, way too close to coming.

"Fuck!"

Dropping both hands from me, she sat back on her heels, her gaze wide. "I'm sorry, I told you I wasn't any good—"

I shook my head, barely resisting the urge to laugh. "Babe, you're fucking perfect. You got me so close to blowing, I'm about to embarrass myself."

Her body had relaxed as I'd spoken, and she now was smiling a sweet little grin as she looked up at me.

"Really?"

"Yeah, babe. I'm not one to bullshit. Ever. I ain't gonna force you to do a damn thing you don't want to, but I might just beg, because, fuck, I need your mouth on me, to know what your tongue and lips on me feel like."

She squirmed, a flush of arousal returning to color her chest, neck and face. I fucking loved that as a redhead, she blushed so easily. Certainly made it even simpler to read her. Leaning forward, she wrapped her palm around my cock as she rested her other one on my thigh like she had earlier. Flicking her gaze up to mine as she licked her lips, she then looked down and swiped her tongue over the tip, lapping up the precum that sat there waiting for her, sending more lightening shooting through me. I had to clench my fists to stop myself from reaching for her, to grip her head and guide her to take me deep.

As much as I wanted to be in her mouth, I knew if I pushed her, I'd fuck this thing up between us. This was as much about building trust as it was about pleasure and learning each other's bodies.

"Fuck, Jacie. You really are a *Ula'ula Mõ'ī*, my fiery red queen. Damn..."

My voice had gone deep, was more gravel than words to the point I wasn't sure she'd have understood what I said. The grin she gave me when she looked up quickly pushed that worry from my mind.

"Finally, you tell me what that actually means. You're lucky I like it."

With a huff, I shook my head, but didn't say a damn thing, not wanting to risk distracting her.

"I love how you taste."

She murmured the words as she returned her focus to my dick, which kicked in her grip at the praise. Moving her hand to the base of my cock, she held me still as she leaned in, mouth open.

Fuck, the sight of her like this, kneeling before me, flushed with arousal, her hands on me, her lips spread wide to take my cock into her mouth for the first time, seared into my brain and I knew I'd remember it until my dying day. Relive it every fucking night. Every time I rubbed one out in the shower would be to thoughts of Jacie in this moment.

Then she rocked my fucking world when she took half my length into her warm mouth on her first glide down.

"Fuck! *Ula'ula Mõ'ī,* Yes..."

Chapter 14

Jacie

The moment I had my lips wrapped around his thick erection, instinct took over and I forgot about being nervous. I loved how his musky scent surrounded me, while his salty-sweet taste coated my tongue. With a hum, I slid down his length, taking as much of him as I could. Strong fingers slid through my hair, making me pause as I worried he'd take control before I was ready, but he didn't do more than continue to run his fingers through my curls, so I got back to sliding up and down his length. Swirling my tongue over the tip each time I pulled back in order to gather all his pre-cum.

After a few more strokes, I got braver, removing my hand from the base of his dick so I could take more of him into my mouth. I hummed as I glided down and joy bubbled within me at his curse and the way his hands tightened in my hair. On my next upstroke I paused to use the tip of my tongue to tease the little notch on the underside of his cock, just below the head, loving how he shuddered in response.

"Fuuuuck..."

The word was more of a groan, a sexy gravelly sound that had my body coming alive, the ache low in my belly increasing until I was squirming. He pulled free from my mouth, tightening his hold in my hair to tilt my face up so I was looking into his dark eyes that shone with how turned on he was.

"Your choice, *Ula'ula Mō'ī*, whether I come down your throat, or toss you on the bed and fuck you hard and fast. But make your decision quick because you got me riding the edge with how fucking sexy you are."

As much as I wanted to know how it felt to swallow him down, my thighs were slick with how needy I was. My core clenched just at the thought of him filling me.

"I need you to fuck me, T. You're not the only one close to that edge."

With a growl, he leaned down and lifted me until I was on my feet. Then nearly faster than I could track, he had my pants undone and down my legs. I'd barely stepped out of the fabric bunched around my ankles when his hands were on my waist, lifting me easily and tossing me onto the mattress. With a squeal I landed on my back but before I could say anything about not being a rag-doll, his hot, sexy as sin body was covering me and his mouth crashed down over mine as he gripped his dick and rubbed the blunt head through my slick folds a moment before he lodged himself at my entrance.

Breaking the kiss, he pushed up on his arms before he thrust his hips forward. I cried out, arching my back while I gripped his shoulders, digging my nails in, in reaction to his sudden invasion. I'd never been with a man Trident's size, and I'd certainly never been with someone with his skills. Choosing to ignore what, or how much, he must have done to be as good as he was, I instead focused on how I was the one lucky enough to be enjoying his talents.

Nuzzling his face in against my neck and shoulder, he pressed a few kisses there before he sucked hard on my skin. The sting of the love-bite added to the other sensations overloading my body and my channel clenched down on his erection. Groaning, he lifted up and, holding my gaze, started to move.

"This is gonna be a hard and fast ride, babe. That sexy mouth of yours has me too fucking close to hold off for long. You tell me if I get too rough."

Spreading my legs wider, I brought my knees up so my feet were flat on the mattress enabling me to move against him, taking him deeper. Loving each tap against my cervix whenever he bottomed out. Sweat slicked both of us and my hands slid from his shoulders as he pounded into me at a frenzied pace. The bed banged against the wall, but neither of us gave a shit. Shifting his weight to one arm, he moved the other down between us, finding my clit easily and teasing the hard little nub. With a gasp, I grabbed for the covers, needing something to hang on to as my body spiraled closer to climax.

"That's it, Ula'ula Mõ'ī, come for me. Let me feel how tight your sweet pussy can clamp down on me while I fill you up."

Fuck, his possessive dirty talk should not be attractive, yet it was. At least in the heat of the moment, it sent another wave of arousal through me, my core rippling around his length. On his next thrust in, I lifted my hips, locking us together as I cried out and came hard enough my vision went black, but not before I felt his dick throb within me, the warmth of his cum filling me and his low curse before his weight dropped on top of me.

When my mind flickered back online Trident was no longer lying over me, instead, he was now propped up on one elbow by my side, tracing patterns over my body with his fingertips. His touch was featherlight, but it was enough to bring my nerves to life and with a moan I squirmed, rubbing my thighs together until I felt the moisture pooling beneath my butt, reminding me that yet again he hadn't used a condom.

Tensing, I reached over and caught his hand with mine, stopping his caresses. His gaze snapped to mine with a frown, like he had no fucking clue why I was glaring at him.

"You didn't use a condom, Trident. *Again.*"

Worry cleared from his expression, which was not what I expected. "Of course I didn't. You're mine, babe. I ain't ever gloving up when I'm fucking my old lady."

With a growl, I released his hand to shove at his chest, rolling him to his back before I sat up, turning to swing my legs over the side of the bed before I looked back at him. Fury had tears stinging my eyes. This man!

"You are un-fucking-believable. How many women have you fucked lately? Dammit, Trident. I've heard stories about how women constantly throw themselves at bikers, how the club whores don't have a say if a man uses a condom or not. I could have caught any number of fucking diseases! And, not that you've fucking asked, but I'm on the Pill so no worries about pregnancy."

As I went to stand his arm banded around my middle and I found myself being hauled back across the bed to where I'd woken up. Pinned down with his large body over me, caging me in, with his face about an inch above my own so I could see just how furious I'd made him. Fear mixed in with my anger, triggering my temper, but before it flared out of control, he started speaking, his voice low and lethal.

"I would *never* fucking risk you like that. Never put you in any sort of danger. I haven't gone without a glove since I was too young and dumb to know any better. Keeping healthy has always been a priority for me, that means I get regular check-ups so I can tell you with certainty that I'm clean. As far as me not asking if you were on the Pill, well, that's because you're my woman, my old lady, and part of that plan is to knock you the fuck up and raise some kids together, yeah? Figure, the sooner I can manage that, the sooner I can stop worrying about if you'll decide to up and ghost me for good one day."

I winced at the reminder over how much I'd hurt him last weekend. "I really am sorry about sneaking out on you like that."

He lowered to drop a kiss on my mouth before returning to his earlier position beside me and trailed his fingers in small circles over my hip, then over to my belly button.

"Dare say it's the universe throwing some fucking karma my way for all the shit I've pulled in the past. But I'm serious about wanting your fucking vow that you won't do it again. We talk shit out, we do not run off and hide."

He tweaked a nipple when I didn't respond straight away.

"Fine! I promise I won't ghost you again. That we'll talk shit out." I didn't voice the "before I leave" that I said to myself, because I wasn't ready to commit for forever. It had only been a bloody week!

He nodded, a satisfied smile curling his lips.

"Oh, and another thing, you'll be wearing an SCMC old lady cut when you head back to Bridgewater. I won't have you running around unpatched."

And just like that my mood was back to black. "Dammit, Trident! No patching me. I'm not a damn bike! I'm a person. No one is gonna own me. *Ever.*"

He sighed, his eyes closing for a minute before he opened them and pinned me with a hard stare.

"Jacie, you knew damn well what accepting my claim would entail. I know you did because your brother has an old lady who wears his patch."

Suddenly feeling way too vulnerable lying naked beside him, I wanted to go find some clothes and get dressed before we had this conversation. But as soon as I went to roll to the side of the bed, his arm shot out over my stomach, pinning me to the mattress as he growled his next words.

"Seriously? You *just* fucking promised me you wouldn't run, that you'd talk to me, and already you're breaking it? You've gotta stop trying to take off every time I say something you don't fucking like, dammit!"

Glaring daggers at him, my body was trembling with my anger. "I wasn't bloody running anywhere! Quit the bullshit caveman routine already. I was just going to clean up and get dressed before we finished talking!"

Between one breath and the next, he had my wrists pinned above my head to the pillow, one in each of his hands. He shifted his body over me, so his bulk pressed me into the mattress. The hot length of his erection nestled against my pussy, sending shards of arousal through me even as fury continued to swirl within me. The smirk he flashed when I instinctively pressed my hips up against him wasn't helping my mood either.

"I prefer you naked, babe. And it has the added benefit that the next time I say somethin' you take offense to, I've got some extra time to catch you before you hit the door. Also, means I can more easily fuck some sense into you once you're done throwing your fit."

I glared fire at him as I twisted and tugged at my wrists. How dare he?

It was my turn to growl some words his way.

"Throwing a fit? Like I'm a fucking toddler. If you think I'll ever let you touch me, let alone fuck me, again after you accuse me of being a damn child when all I want is not to be *owned*, you're fucking nuts."

He huffed out a breath. "You really got a chip on your shoulder about your age, huh? You might be several years younger than me, babe, but trust me, I'm well aware you're all woman. Never once have I thought you were a child, no matter what endearment I call you. Hell, half the time I call my brothers boys and they're all grown ass men."

I clenched my jaw at his logical point. No one seemed to be able to understand how frustrating it was to not only be constantly referred to as Taz's "baby sister", but to also be treated like I was still a little kid. I was a fully trained AFP operative, dammit! And I hadn't been a child since the day my father had murdered my mother and lit the fire that was meant to take my life. So yeah, I got a little mad whenever I was accused of acting like a kid. Since I didn't think Trident would be any different from any of the other bikers I'd attempted to explain it to, I figured it would be a waste of time to try with Trident now.

"Well, just stop calling me girlie or accusing me of having a *fit* and things will go a lot smoother. But I'm serious about not wearing anything that has the words 'property of' on it."

Closing his eyes on a sigh he pressed his forehead against mine, our noses touching briefly, before he lifted back up. "Jacie, being a biker's property, his old lady, ain't like you're a fucking table or something. It means you belong to me, and me to you."

He paused and flexed his hips, rubbing his erection through my wet folds and making me shudder beneath him.

"Considering how wet you are, I'm thinking you don't mind belonging to me. Being mine. So let's get this outta the way. A biker doesn't patch his woman because he thinks she's a possession. It's because she is his center: the most precious, important part of his heart and soul. You'll wear my cut so that everyone will see my name and know whose protection you have. Who will be the last man they see before they leave this world if they're fucking stupid enough to mess with for you. Putting my patch on you is about protecting you, keeping you safe. Along with declaring to the world how much of a lucky bastard I am to have such a feisty, kickass woman in my bed and life."

As much as I hadn't wanted to understand, his speech had softened me to the concept. But I still had an issue with the wordage. "Does it really *have* to say 'property of'?"

He chuckled and flexed his hips again, making me bite the inside of my cheek to prevent a moan from escaping.

"Oh, that's staying. You are totally gonna be my property, babe. But not how you're thinkin'. You're thinking civilian, but you're in the MC world now, you gotta think about it from that perspective. You are the thing I cherish most in this world, even more important than my Harley. You're my ride or die, the one I will *always* stand in front of to protect."

Tears pricked my eyes at this romantic side of him. Even if it was biker style and possessive as hell. Before he had me bawling, I lifted up and kissed him to shut him up. He chuckled against my lips before shifting his hips back until the head of his dick lined up with my entrance. Releasing my wrists, he lowered down to continue kissing me as he slowly slid inside me.

Wrapping my arms around his neck, I held him to me as he proceeded to claim me all over again.

Chapter 15

Trident

Jacie's friends pounding on the adjoining door at midnight wasn't how I'd planned on waking up. Hoping I could at least save Jacie from being disturbed, I rushed to pull my jeans on as I moved over toward the sound. I should have realized it was pointless to even try. Before I could flip the lock, Jacie was calling out from behind me.

"Shut the hell up already!"

The moment I had the door open, the three girls burst into the room.

"Whoa. Damn." The oldest of her friends stalled out in front of me, running her gaze up and down as she shook her head. I couldn't resist flexing a little—I was only human, and while I was a one woman man and completely committed to Jacie, I wasn't immune to enjoying when another chick was admiring me.

"Geez, Neveah, take a photo why don't you?" One of the other girls, I was fairly certain her name was Sparrow, said as she grabbed Neveah's arm and tugged her over toward the bed. Where Jacie was now sitting up, nothing but the thin hotel sheet covering her sexy tits while she glared daggers at me.

My eyes widened. "What? Did you not want me to let them in?"

Those pretty blue irises of hers rolled before returning to send fire my way.

"Don't think I failed to notice what you just did. Makes me think our earlier conversation was nothing but a bunch of lies. Typical bloody bloke. Say anything to get into a woman's knickers. Go, Trident, and leave me the fuck alone."

I was speechless for a few moments as I tried to figure out how I'd gone from waking up happily wrapped around my woman to her kicking me out minutes later.

"Jacie, I didn't fucking lie to you about a damn thing. Wanna explain what the fuck you're so worked up about?"

Tugging the sheet free from the mattress as she shuffled over to the edge of the bed, she made fast work of wrapping the fabric around her before she stormed over to me.

"You were totally putting on a show for Neveah just now. Don't you dare try to deny it! I saw you flex your arms and pecs. You do that to every chick that looks your way? I'm just one of many, aren't I?"

Motherfucker! Tears shone in her eyes, tearing me to my soul. I reached for her but she danced out of range.

"Babe, I wasn't fucking lying when I said I wanted to be exclusive, but I'm only human. A pretty girl stops to stare at my muscles, I can't help but enjoy the moment. Doesn't mean I'd even think about wanting to take shit further! You telling me you don't get a buzz outta men stopping to check you out when you go out all dolled up?"

The fire that flickered in her gaze had me wincing. Guess not.

"Women do not like strange men ogling them. Ever. It's creepy."

I raised an eyebrow as Neveah spun to glare at her friend. "Uh, Jacie, did you just call me creepy because I happened to notice Trident takes *very* good care of himself?"

She spun to face her friend. "Well, it wasn't exactly polite! Just wait till you get a man and we all start flirting with him."

Scrubbing a hand over my face before tugging on my beard, I growled in frustration. Which drew my woman's attention back my way.

"Oh, please. Don't you dare start with some alpha macho bullshit. You just flirted with my friend. In front of me. Nope. You need to go."

She then stormed over to the bathroom and locked herself in. I blinked in shock, not sure what to do. My first instinct was to kick the door down to get to my woman, but I rather suspected that would get hotel security called on me, if not the cops. No matter which way I went, I was going to be leaving without her.

With another growl I stomped over to where our clothes were and finished getting dressed before I glanced at her three friends.

"I'll be back tomorrow." I pointed at Neveah. "You need to fix this shit you started. I'm not gonna lose my old lady because she's fucking jealous over nothing."

Before any of them could say a thing in response, I was out the door and stomping down the hallway in a helluva mood.

Should have known better than to believe I could get Jacie pinned down and fully on board with being my old lady so soon. My woman had one hell of a temper, even for a redhead. While I took a slither of joy that, with how jealous she got over such a small thing, it meant she cared. Her reaction to it was way over the top. No way was I gonna stand for that sort of bullshit drama from her going forward.

Tomorrow I'd be finding a way to be alone with her to straighten out some rules. She was fucking mine. I wasn't ever going to want another woman. She needed to get that clear.

Entering the lobby, I spotted Stone and headed his way. He raised an eyebrow as I approached.

"What the fuck happened, brother?"

With a glare, I didn't bother answering his query.

"I'm riding out. Catch you later."

"Whoa." He reached to grip my bicep, then moved us away from the ladies he'd been chatting with. "Seriously, Trident. Tell me what the fuck happened? Figured things were good with how long you were gone."

I shook my head. "Nothing I wanna talk about. I'm out. Catch you later, brother."

Pulling free from his grip, I stormed outside and quickly got on my bike and left the parking lot. Needing to vent, to calm the fuck down, I took the more scenic route to Cutler. Skipping the clubhouse, I instead went to my place. I cut the engine as I pulled up and was about to unlock the door when my phone rung with the tone I'd set for Viper.

"Yeah Prez?"

"You still in Dallas?"

"Nah, just got to my place. What's up?"

"Need you in my office ASAP."

The line went dead before I could say another word. But that wasn't unusual for Viper. With a sigh, I turned back toward my ride. Looked like I wasn't getting anything I fucking wanted tonight: not sleeping beside my old lady, or having time to work out my frustrations on my latest project in the shed before enjoying a beer or two.

Arriving at the clubhouse, I gave the prospect manning the gate a nod. Parking my bike in the line up, I jogged up the stairs, passed the prospect on the entrance with a chin dip, then headed inside. Going straight for the rear hallway, I didn't stop until I came to the open doorway of Viper's office, where I paused before entering.

"You wanted to see me, Prez?"

He looked up from his laptop. "Yeah, come in and shut the fucking door."

I did as I was told, then sat in the chair in front of his desk. Resisted the urge to ask what was going on. Viper would tell me when he was good and ready.

"Any truth to the rumors I'm hearing about you and Taz's baby sister."

I clenched my fists beneath the desk as I tried to not growl at my president. Suddenly I had a better understanding of my woman's issue with how everyone viewed her. If everyone did what Viper had just done when they spoke about her, or to her, it made sense. I'd be mad as hell over it if I were in her place, that's for sure.

"Jacie's twenty-six fucking years old, Viper. Not exactly a kid, yeah?"

With a shake of his head, he chuckled. "I'll just take that as a yes then."

I scrubbed a hand over my face before giving my beard a tug. Viper was a hard-ass, but he wasn't a monster, he'd not meant any harm with what he'd said. Forcing myself to calm the fuck down, I gave Viper the answer he'd wanted.

"Yeah, Prez. I've claimed her. Well, been trying to. She keeps agreeing to be mine, then losing her damn mind and kicking me to the curb."

That got me another chuckle from my president. "You always did like a challenge. But I'm not sure you're ready for the kind you'll get from a red head, brother. Especially a fiery Australian one. Let me know when you're ready to make it public and I'll order her property patch."

"Order it now. I'll get her in it even if I have to wrestle her into the thing. I'll declare it next time we have church, assuming you're good with that?"

His gaze went glacial, putting me on alert. "You need to have her total agreement, Trident. You can't force a woman to be your old lady. That's not how that works. Not under my watch."

And that was one of the reasons Viper was an excellent President. We might be a one percenter club and run drugs, guns and do various other illegal things, but human trafficking, coercing women into doing something they didn't want, was a hard line he wouldn't allow the club to cross.

"Yeah, I know. And you know I wouldn't want a woman if I had to force her. Jacie's just taking some convincing to agree to the life of being a biker's old lady."

He gave me a nod, "All right then, I'll order her patches in."

"Ah, about that, any way we could do a rush order?"

Pinching the bridge of his nose, he frowned. "Do you know more than I do about the danger coming her way?"

With those words, I instantly forgot all about getting my patch on her. Doubting he'd be this dramatic about the shit Animal had pulled with her last weekend, I leaned forward, elbows on my knees, and locked my gaze onto my president's.

"If I'd known something was coming for her, I never would have left her back at the hotel. What danger are you talking about?"

"Got a call from Scout earlier. The Charon president was in a helluva state. He doesn't know about you and her, by the way. He rung me to call in the favor he says we owe his club for what happened to Flick."

I shrugged a shoulder. "With it being Jacie in danger, it makes no difference. She's my fucking woman. I'll protect her regardless. You know what's coming her way?"

"Figured that's how you'd feel. Taz got a call from Frank, Jacie's adopted dad, apparently he's Australia Federal Police, so have fun with that for your in-laws. Anyhow, he rung to warn that Jacie's got trouble coming for her. Seems her biological father's brother, Terrence Milani, had thought she was dead along with everyone else. Now he's learned she's alive, he's coming her way and Frank believes he intends to snatch her. Scout wants us to make sure she stays safe while she's in Dallas, then to escort her and the other girls — Neveah, Sparrow and Mirabelle — back to Bridgewater after the event is done tomorrow. There are a Charon brother and prospect shadowing them, but Taz is demanding more coverage than what they can provide."

While I had no problem keeping my woman and her friends safe, a few things weren't adding up.

"Why didn't Frank call her directly? Tell her to get her ass back to Bridgewater. While she might be stubborn as hell, she's not stupid, if she knew her uncle was after her, she'd cancel the trip and head back to her brother for the club's protection."

"Jacie's phone is off, which is why Frank rung Taz. Guessing you might have something to do with that?"

I cleared my throat as my cheeks heated. "I may have fired up her temper before I left. That doesn't explain why they're not blowing up the other girls' cells."

"Scout tells me Keys checked the locaters on all of their phones, and they're all in their hotel rooms. The prospects are on alert for the uncle, but they haven't seen him yet. Scout said they decided not to wake the girls up just to tell them to be careful. He mentioned something about being worried about Sparrow getting hold of a gun."

Keys was the Charon MC's tech guy. Man was a fucking genius with computers, and had a thing with needing to keep those around him safe. The club had recently started a new company "Athena Security", which had given the man an even bigger budget and more manpower to get shit done.

I rubbed a hand over my face. "Yeah, he's right to worry. Whoever ends up with that girl has my sympathy. She's already one helluva handful. So, why isn't Taz racing up here with a Charon crew?"

"Flick nearly lost their baby last week. He can't leave her, and Scout rightfully pointed out that it made more sense to call us in since we could get brothers there faster than they could. At a guess, they'll still send a crew up. That hotel is gonna look like a biker convention, not a book one."

It was my turn to laugh. "You haven't actually looked into the event at all, have you? Trust me, those ladies will be in seventh heaven if they wake up to find the place filled with bikers. Might want to warn the men that they'll be mobbed. The event's called Motorcycles, Mobsters and Mayhem. No one's gonna think anything's out of place if a bunch of extra bikers turn up."

Viper looked at me dumbfounded a few minutes before mumbling under his breath something about insanity. Normally I'd tease him some more, but knowing my old lady was in danger had me on edge, needing to get back to her.

"Know what he wants with her?"

"No. Scout wouldn't tell me more over the phone. Got the feeling it wasn't anything good. How much you know about your girl? You got any ideas?"

I snorted. "Well, I know not to call her a girl if I want to stay standing. But seriously, we haven't exactly had time to get into our pasts. No fucking clue who her family is beyond Taz."

Viper growled. "I fucking hate being in the dark. Get me more info ASAP on what the fuck this Milani bastard wants with your woman. You good to head back to the hotel?"

I was on my feet before he'd finished speaking. "Fuck yeah, I am. I'll go pack some clothes and weapons then head out."

"Good deal. I'll get hold of Stone and let him know to back you up. Then after the fucking sun rises, I'll send more brothers that way to help. Before you run out of here, give me her room number and I'll call the hotel and get you a room as close to theirs as I can while you're heading in."

After giving it to him, I was through his door and jogging up the stairs in record time. Ten minutes after I left Viper's office, I was back on my bike, roaring out of the clubhouse parking lot and heading back toward Dallas.

Instead of pulling up out the front like earlier, I made my way around to the hotel's covered parking garage and chose a spot in an out of the way corner. Didn't need Jacie seeing my ride and ghosting on me again.

It didn't take long for me to get checked in and up to the fourth floor. I stopped outside her door, pressing my palm to the painted timber, wishing like hell I could check she was in there safe and sound. But knew that wasn't a good idea. With how her temper had flared earlier, I was pretty sure she'd need some time to cool off before she saw me again. I also doubted she would have gone anywhere after I left. With a sigh I turned to my room that was opposite hers. Once inside, and after I'd completed my usual checks, I sat on the bed and stared out the window at Dallas all lit up and prayed Jacie wouldn't give me too much hell in the morning.

Chapter 16

Jacie

I'd set an alarm to vibrate my smart watch last night to make sure I woke up before Nevaeh did. Being careful to not make much noise, I slipped from my bed and got dressed before I grabbed my handbag and crept out of our hotel room. I mentally shook my head as I padded down the hallway. This was now two weekends in a row I'd snuck out of a room to slip away from someone sleeping. This was getting to be a habit, one I didn't want.

I'd already been freaking out last night over Trident's determination to claim me as his old lady. It was way too soon. Being a biker's old lady was like being his wife, for fuck's sake. We'd known each other a bloody week. When he'd started preening for Nevaeh, I'd lost it. My temper flared and as per usual, my mouth ran away on me.

Dashing at the moisture in my eyes, I made my way down the hallway toward the elevator. Nevaeh hadn't said a word after my outburst. Once I'd come out of the bathroom, she'd gone in. Returning changed in her PJs, she then climbed into her bed and, facing away from me, went to sleep. Sparrow and Mirabelle had thrown me the same treatment. When I tried to talk to them, after Neveah had gone into the bathroom, they'd just shaken their heads and returned to their room. Closing the door behind them.

Some fucking birthday. Seemed I should have taken the bloody hint last weekend that I wasn't meant to celebrate this year, and canceled this trip. I could be home right now playing with Lolly. And still have my three best friends. Instead, I'd pushed away a man I actually liked, even if he was moving way too fast and was possessive as hell, and hurt my besties to a point I feared I'd lost their friendship. Dashing more tears from my face, I exited onto the ground floor and headed directly for the exit, not bothering to look around the lobby. I had zero desire to chat with other readers or models, or even worse, any SCMC brothers that were no doubt still lurking around this morning.

Pulling my sunglasses from my bag, I slid them on as I left the hotel and made my way down the footpath. Finding a quirky looking cafe, one I was certain no self-respecting biker would ever be seen dead in, I ducked in. Removing my sunglasses, I looked over their menu, happy to see they had one of my favorites. Stepping up to the queue at the counter, I took in the woman serving.

At a guess, she was in her early thirties, and she had her long, straight hair tied back in a ponytail. The lower half was dyed an emerald green, while the top half a bright blue; I could imagine how cool it would look with the underneath color peaking through as she moved when it wasn't tied back. Along with the several small hoop earrings in each ear, she had a star shaped silver stud in the left side of her nose and a ring through the center of her lower lip. Her eyes had a splash of green eye shadow that matched her hair, and black winged eyeliner that was so perfectly even, I was in awe of her skill. I didn't often bother with makeup, so I was far from an expert. I had tried to apply wings a few times so I knew how bloody hard they were to master. I'd gotten so frustrated every time I'd tried, I'd ended up cleaning my attempts off and not even bothering with eyeliner.

If the cafe wasn't so busy, I might have asked her how she did it but there were already three people lined up behind me so I didn't take up any more of the woman's time than I needed to. With a smile, I ordered myself a cappuccino, with almond milk, along with a ham and cheese sourdough sandwich, toasted. With a smile, I took the stand she gave me with a table number on it before I headed to the booth in the back corner I'd spotted when I'd come in. Once I'd gotten comfortable on the bench seat, I pulled out my phone and tapped the screen, out of habit. When it stayed black, I remembered how I'd turned it off last night so Trident couldn't try to call me after I'd kicked him out. Chewing my lower lip, I stared at the black screen trying to decide if I should turn it on or not. With a mental shake of my head, I decided against it. I was already hanging by a thread, no way could I handle anything else. Whether it came from Trident, one of my girls, Flick or Taz. Tucking it back into my handbag, I pulled out my notepad instead. I was hoping that journaling down my thoughts would help clear my mind; it might even give me some damn clarity on what I should do about it all, or how to at least fix my friendships.

Holding my pen, the page remained blank. I had no idea where to even start. The scent of freshly brewed coffee hit me moments before my order was placed beside me.

"Here you go. Enjoy."

Before I could respond the waitress was gone, off to collect the next order. Setting my pen down, I wrapped my palms around the warm mug, closing my eyes to inhale the aroma. *Hmm, so good.* Leaving it to cool down a bit more before I drunk it, I moved to pick up my toasted sandwich. Nearly moaning out loud after I took my first bite, it was that good. Not too hot, with the perfect ratio of ham to cheese to bread.

As I continued to eat, I let my thoughts wander, and paused to jot down some notes as I did, that was until I spotted Animal coming my way. Having just finished my food, I tidied up, putting away my notebook while making it look like I was just clearing things off to enjoy my coffee. I didn't want anyone reading my private thoughts and notes, especially not Animal.

With my mug between both my palms, I lifted it to begin taking sips as I watched him come closer. With how pale and sickly he looked, and the way he flexed and tapped his fingers against his thigh as he walked between tables, I had to agree with Trident's guess that the man was hooked on something, and it looked like he hadn't had a fix yet this morning. He held my gaze as he moved around to the side of my table, his eyes were red rimmed, and his pupils didn't look right. I frowned when he slid into the seat beside me as though we were good friends. He sniffled then cleared his throat as he shuffled in the seat to face me. My temper flared at his brazenness, and I set my drink down to help resist the urge I had to pour it over his head.

"Ah, what do you think you're doing?"

He gave me a sleazy grin he no doubt thought was sexy.

"Saw you in here and figured I'd stop in for a little chat, hot stuff."

Oh jeez, and to think I complained about Trident calling me girlie. I'd take that any day over 'hot stuff'.

"And what exactly would we have to talk about,

Animal? Last I heard, you'd put a bet out on my demise."

He huffed out a laugh and reached for my drink, picking it up and downing half of it in one gulp.

Sitting up straighter, I glared daggers his way. "What the fuck? Get your own damn drink if you want one."

Ignoring my comment, he banged the mug down with a grimace. "What the fuck did they do to your coffee? Whatever the fuck that shit is, it should be illegal."

I rolled my eyes, not giving two shits that he didn't like my choice in beverage.

"It's got almond milk in it. I like how it tastes. Now, why the fuck are you here bothering me? Wouldn't have thought you'd be an early riser, especially not on a Saturday."

He shrugged a shoulder, and I expected him to spout off some bullshit, but instead he winced and hunched to his right, an arm banded across his middle, his hand going under his cut.

Frowning, some of my anger dissipated to be replaced with concern. No matter how much of a douchebag the guy was, if he was unwell, I'd try to help him. It just wasn't in my nature to let anyone suffer.

"Animal? You okay? If you're not feeling great, we can go to the hospital, or I could ring Trident. Your club has a doctor, right? We can get you help."

At least I'd heard of a SCMC brother called Doc. While it was one helluva assumption that the bloke had medical skills, considering Animal was most likely just strung out with withdrawals, it wasn't like he needed some top-notch specialist. More like rehab, but I doubted that would go over well if I suggested it. The guy clearly had one hell of a male ego going on.

With another sniff, he straightened and gave me a forced smile. "Nah, last thing we need is your guard dog to roll up on us. But if you could help me out to my bike, I'd appreciate it."

Drumming my fingers on my thigh under the table for a moment, I tried to puzzle out what he was up to. No way did he need my help to get outside. And why'd he come in here in the first place if he wanted to leave already? Nope. He was up to something.

"Considering we're not exactly friends, Animal, and you've been talking enough shit about what you wanna do to me that I've heard about it, I think I'll just stay here. Don't mistake my wanting to get you help for stupidity. Clearly you're craving whatever poison you've gotten hooked on, so, I'll call in your club brothers, or a cab to take you to the hospital. But that's it. I'm not—"

Shock had me stilling when, with a low growl, he slid over until he was pressed against me, suddenly full of rage. A moment later, he'd pulled out the gun that had been holstered on his belt and jammed the muzzle into my ribs, keeping it all hidden behind the table from the rest of the cafe. Why had I thought being in the back corner was a good idea? My blood ran cold as a shiver tripped down my spine when I looked him in the eye. Keeping my gaze steady, I refused to let him see the fear that was churning inside me.

"What—"

He shoved the gun harder into me, until I grunted with a wince. "Shut the fuck up and listen, you little bitch. You don't gotta worry about nothing but doing what you're told, understand?"

Tears pricked my eyes as I nodded.

"'Bout fucking time. No clue how Trident stands all the chatter. Now, you're going to stick real close to me as we head out the back door. Try anything and I'll shoot you. Gut shot is a nasty way to die, but that's what you'll be choosing if you pull any sorta stunt. And don't think that because we're in public that'll stop me. It won't. The SCMC hold enough power in Dallas no one will interfere, and I'll be long gone before any cop can make it here."

With that, he pulled back, tucking his hand holding the gun under the leather of his cut, out of sight. Although, I didn't need to be able to see it to know he still had it aimed my way, that he wasn't joking when he said he'd shoot me. Grabbing my handbag, I scooted across the bench seat until I could stand, then I walked with him as he'd instructed, toward the hallway that was opposite where I'd been sitting. The sign above the entrance announced that the bathrooms along with the exit to the rear parking lot were this way. Since it was an area customers were allowed to use, it meant that, unfortunately, no one even glanced our way as we headed in that direction.

Once we'd left the main cafe area and were alone in the narrow hall, he stopped bothering to hide his weapon. Instead, he kept the muzzle pressed to my lower back as I led the way toward the exit. My mind spun, trying to think of a way I could to break away from him without coming up with much. I just hoped that once we were outside in the open, I'd get an opportunity to escape.

Once we passed through the door, shock had me stumbling to a stop when I saw who was waiting for us, and any hope I'd had of finding a way out died.

"No fucking way."

Terrence Milani should be back in Melbourne where the bastard belonged. Well, he really should be rotting in prison for all he'd done, but since he was a well-connected arsehole, I'd accepted that him being on the other side of the planet far away from me was as good as I was going to get when it came to him.

Animal digging that gun muzzle into my spine had me wincing. "Keep moving. Don't have all day."

Walking toward the man I hadn't seen since I was a toddler, rather felt like I was being led toward the devil. I'd never liked Uncle Terrence, neither had Mum, but Dad had hero worshiped his older brother and would do any damn thing the man told him to do.

My uncle looked basically the same as I remembered; stylish, wearing tailored dress pants, shirt with no tie and the top few buttons undone, all black, including his shoes. Although, he had some silver at his temples now that hadn't been there when I'd been a kid.

As we approached, he straightened from where he'd been leaning against a big black SUV. "Well, as I live and breathe, if it isn't my precious little niece, back from the dead."

I clenched my fists, wanting to punch him in his smug face so badly, it was hard to resist taking a swing at him. While my dad had been the one to murder my mother, it was Uncle Terrence who was the reason I'd been placed into witness protection, not allowed to contact my brother. They'd forced me to change my name from Grace Milani to Jacie Lewis. To move so far away from where I'd grown up that I'd never even been able to visit my mum's grave.

"What the fuck do you want? Why all this cloak and dagger bullshit?"

He frowned with a shake of his head. "Such language, Grace. You'll need to stop cussing like that. He won't like it, and keeping him happy is going to be your new life's purpose."

I faked a nonchalance I definitely was not feeling

and rolled my eyes. "All you're gonna give me is a '*he*', really? More fucking vague bullshit. Not that it matters, because it'll be a cold day in hell before I willingly go anywhere with you."

Holding my glare with a raised eyebrow, he grinned, a big toothy shark's smile that had my heart rate pounding as I wondered what the fuck he was about to do. After watching me squirm for a few moments, his expression grew serious and his focus shifted to my left. "You took her phone like I ordered you to?"

Animal grunted, "Yeah, tossed it in the trash can inside. You want me to go get it?"

Keeping my expression exactly the same, I kept my gaze on my uncle, the biggest threat here, while I wondered what Animal was playing at with his lie. Terrence frowned with a huff before shaking his head.

"No, leave it where it is, and if you want your precious pills, you need to complete the job."

Too late I realized I should have been watching Animal, not my uncle. I managed to turn far enough to see the gun butt coming toward me, but had no time to avoid it. Pain flared like fire through me as Animal slammed the weapon against the top of my head. As I crumpled to the ground my uncle growled out an order, but I couldn't make out any words before darkness took me.

Chapter 17

Trident

Rising just after sunup, I rushed to shower then propped open my door so I'd be able to hear when Jacie, or any of the girls, came out of their rooms while I finished getting ready. I was drinking the last mouthful of my first cup of coffee for the day when my cell phone rang. Seeing it was Stone, I accepted the call, frowning when, before I had the thing to my ear, I could hear him yelling.

"Where the fuck are you?"

I had no clue what was going on, but the sirens I could hear in the background had me worried. "I'm at the hotel, waiting for Jacie to wake up. Why? And where the hell are you?"

"She ain't there, brother. Some suit just snatched her from a parking lot two blocks down from the hotel."

In seconds I was in front of Jacie's room, pounding my fist on the door as I responded to Stone.

"What the fuck do you mean she was snatched?"

Nevaeh opened the door before I finished speaking, her expression filling with fear as she silently stepped aside to let me pass. I rushed in, hoping somehow Stone was wrong but Jacie's empty bed dashed that hope.

Stone's tone was harsh, like he was blaming me for this shit. "I mean, I just saw her get pistol-whipped and tossed into the back of a SUV, brother."

The sirens in the background continued to get louder, forcing me to yell to make sure he'd hear me.

"Tell me you're following them."

He growled back at me, fury clear in his tone. "I couldn't fucking follow her because I'm busy trying to keep enough of Animal's blood inside his body so the dumb fuck doesn't die on us. Why the fuck weren't you with her? Thought you were meant to be on her ass twenty-four/seven."

Nothing about this was making sense. Why would Jacie have gotten up at the crack of dawn? Because that's how early she'd have to have left for me to have not seen or heard her go. The sirens finally cut out.

"I gotta go. Call Viper and get after her, Trident. I'll handle Animal."

Nevaeh lowered her phone and tears tracked down her cheeks as she stared at Sparrow. "Her phone's off. How are we gonna find her?"

Sparrow's jaw clenched and she got a determined look in her gaze that I could appreciate. That girl had a core of steel and would not hesitate to do whatever was needed to help find her friend. "I've got an idea."

After dialing her cell she lifted it to her ear and looked me in the eye as she spoke into it. "Hey Keys. Jacie's been taken and her phone's off. Can you track her?"

She lowered her gaze with a wince, and I could just hear his voice so I knew he was yelling.

"I don't know what happened, Keys! All I know is she's gone and I have Trident here up in my grill."

Just as someone started knocking on the door she strode up to me. "He wants to talk to you."

"Hey Keys. Just a sec." Pulling the phone from my mouth I called out to Sparrow who'd headed to the entrance of the room. "Don't open that fucking door!"

Keys pulled my attention back to him. "It's fine Trident, it's a couple of our guys. Jazz and Gypsy, good guys. Solid. They've been tailing the girls since they left Bridgewater. Tell me what happened."

Good thing they were friendlies because Sparrow had ignored me and opened the door to let in two men. When I saw they were both indeed wearing Charon MC colors, I focused back on Keys.

"Not one hundred percent sure. I was in the room across from the girls. Been up since the sun rose waiting for them to leave their rooms, but somehow missed Jacie leaving. Stone just called me, told me a suit snatched her from a parking lot two blocks down from the hotel. Only other details were that she was pistol-whipped and tossed into a black SUV, and he's still there trying to stop Animal from bleeding out. He ended the call when the ambulance arrived. That's all I got."

"Damn. Fuck. Okay, her phone is off, so I can't get her location right away. So long as it doesn't have a flat battery, I'll work on seeing if I can get around that to get the location, but I can't promise it'll work. That's assuming she still has it with her. I've got Arrow here looking through the CCTV cameras outside the hotel to track her that way. Any idea on a time she would have left?"

"More than half hour ago if she left before I was up, which she must have been or I would have heard her leave."

"Right. I normally do a little something else to keep our women and kids safe, but Jacie's too fucking smart for her own good. Didn't take her long to find and ditch them. I'll keep you posted when we know anything. You do the same, yeah?"

"Definitely. Talk soon."

As soon as I ended the call, Sparrow had her hand out for her phone. Before I handed it over, I texted Keys' number to myself. As she took it from me, I nodded toward the back corner of the room where one of the Charon's men were kneeling in front of Mirabelle, who had curled into a ball on the floor, half hidden by the curtains. Her body rocked while she chewed at her thumb-nail. Lost within her mind, she appeared completely oblivious to the man beside her, or anything else. With the vacant look in her eyes, one that I'd seen on my brother's faces who were struggling with flashbacks, I guessed she was having some sort of PTSD episode.

"What's up with her?"

Sparrow glanced over with a wince. "Not my story to tell. Just know all of this is flipping a whole lot of Mirabelle's triggers. Gypsy'll take care of her." She turned back to me. "What did Keys say? He tracking her?"

I shook my head, "You know her phone is either turned off or flat, that's assuming she even has it. What makes you think Keys could track her?"

A blush pinkened her cheeks as she cleared her throat, but when she went to speak again, Jazz stepped in close to her. "Sparrow, shut it. You know better than to share club secrets like that."

The fire that filled her gaze as she turned on the idiot had my heart aching with how it reminded me of Jacie. Fuck, where was my woman right now?

I didn't bother telling the little Charon bastard that since I was SCMC I outranked him, and that he had to tell me whatever the fuck I ordered him to. Keys had told me enough for me to know he obviously somehow low-jacked the club's women and kids. It was a good fucking idea, and one I'd be bringing up at Church for us to replicate. Plus, I didn't need to rip the guy a new one because Sparrow was already taking care of that. Ignoring the two of them, I paced while I sent a text to Viper. Keeping it brief, I let him know that Stone was with Animal on the way to hospital and that Jacie had been taken. Also told him that Keys was working on getting her location, and I was waiting with the remaining Charon crew until I heard back from him.

Tilting my neck each way to stretch it out, I cursed. I fucking hated the waiting. Knowing my woman needed me, I was willing and able to do whatever was necessary to save her, but without even a general direction to head in, I couldn't do much. And it was fucking killing me. When my phone buzzed I didn't even check caller ID before I had it to my ear.

"Trident."

"This is Taz."

Well, fuck. Like I needed to deal with Jacie's overprotective brother on top of everything else right now.

"You got any news for me?"

"Yeah, right after you tell me what my sister is to you."

I growled, and if he'd been in front of me I'd have had him pinned to the wall by the throat.

"She's my fucking old lady and we do *not* have time for a pissing match right now. Tell me what you know or fuck off."

He huffed a laugh. "Yeah, that's the attitude you'll need with my baby sis."

I didn't let him say another word. "You need to cut

that shit out already. You know how big a chip on her shoulder she has about her age because everyone keeps fucking calling her your baby sis? She's a grown ass adult. Now, quit wasting my fucking time. You got a location on her yet?"

He was silent for a moment, like he didn't appreciate being put in his place, but whatever, I'd deal with his bruised ego later.

"No location yet. Arrow tracked her from the hotel to a cafe up the street." Ice edged his tone. "Got into the cameras in the parking lot, the fucker that took her is her uncle. Terrence Milani, he's a mid-level mobster in Melbourne, thinks he's big time, but hasn't ever quite managed to make it beyond mid-level. Camera showed Animal bringing her out at gunpoint. They spoke for a few minutes before Animal cracked her over the head with the butt of his gun—just like he fucking did to my woman. As his men were grabbing Jacie, Terrence put a bullet into Animal's shoulder." He paused and I could hear a muffled conversation before Taz returned to me. "Motherfucking bastard! He took her to a private airfield. I'll call back when we get the flight plan."

"I'll get a crew and be at the airport ready to go as soon as you get that location."

I hung up before he could bitch me out about how he should be the one to go get her. It made no difference to me if he was going or not, I was gonna get my woman back. Dialing Viper, I turned to see everyone, except Mirabelle, staring my way.

"Her uncle's the one that snatched her, bastard's taken her to a private airstrip. I'll be flying out after her as soon as I have a fucking location." I pinned first Jazz then Gypsy with my gaze. "You two need to get these three back to Bridgewater. Doubt they're in danger now this Terrence Milani bastard has left town, but it ain't worth the risk. Get them home. That's an order."

Without giving them time to respond, I strode out and crossed the hallway to my room. I tossed the few things I'd pulled from my bag back into it as I called Viper to update him and request he send a couple of brothers to meet me at the airport.

Jacie

Muttering a curse, I rubbed my temples trying to ease the mother of all headaches that had woken me.

"Welcome back to the land of the living, niece."

Letting out a breath, memories flooded back of how Animal had handed me over to my uncle before knocking me out. Moving a hand to the back of my head, I gently prodded the lump that had formed where the fucker had clocked me. Grateful when I didn't find any blood, wet or dried around it.

I didn't need to open my eyes to know I was on a plane, and with the way I could feel the slight tilt and shift of the aircraft, knew it was in the air. Still, when I lifted my lids to take in my surroundings, the opulence of the private plane was an unexpected shock. Although, I probably should have expected it considering my uncle was involved. He'd always believed he deserved the best of the best.

Zeroing my gaze in on my piece of shit uncle, I bit the inside of my cheek to stop myself rolling my eyes at how much of a fucking stereotype mobster he was. Sitting opposite me, he was lounging comfortably in his fancy fucking seat, with a crystal glass of amber liquid in his hand, swirling the whiskey like he owned the fucking world. He chuckled with a small shake of his head when my gaze narrowed to a glare.

"Look at you, as fiery as your mother was in the beginning. But just like her, you'll be tamed soon enough."

Fury flashed hot through me at him speaking of my mother like that. "Your brother fucking murdered her. If that's what you mean by 'tamed', I think I'll pass and stay wild."

A flash of rage passed over his features. "Gordon is a loose cannon, always has been. It's why he was never brought into the family business beyond doing some wet work. Him killing your mother was not part of my plan. Quite the opposite in fact. It actually left me in quite the predicament, one I can finally resolve now I've reacquired you."

Every word he spoke had my hatred for him increasing.

"If he was such a pain in the arse, why didn't you have him taken out when he was in prison?"

He gave me another of his shark smiles. I didn't like it anymore now than I had earlier. "Because that would have been over too quickly. I wanted him to suffer."

With a frown, I took a moment to think over what he'd just told me.

"Bullshit. He wouldn't have gotten out early for good behavior if you'd made life hard for him inside. Nah, I'm guessing the truth was more like he wasn't worth the effort, or losing the favors you'd have had to pull in, to get to him. And then. once he was out, you could force him to do whatever you wanted with the threat of torturing him for what he'd done."

Now he was the one frowning. "You're too smart for your own good, Grace. Such a pity you were born a girl.

Had you been a boy, I'd have been able to groom you to take my place." With a shake of his head, he lifted the crystal glass to take a sip. "If he ever shows his face again, I can guarantee he won't survive long. He'd been given a job to do, to get back into the family's good graces, but instead of doing it, he fled the country and vanished."

It took effort to keep my face the same, to not give away the fact that my bastard of a sperm donor was already dead and gone; to contain how much I wanted to laugh at how my uncle was going to continue to waste his time and money searching for a dead man.

Turning to look out of the window beside me, my mouth went dry when I caught glimpses of the ocean between all the clouds below us.

"Where are you taking me? Back to Australia?"

Panic had my heart racing as my mind swirled with possibilities, which did not help my headache.

"I'll be heading home eventually, but first we're making a stop in Kauai to drop you off."

Closing my eyes, I rubbed my fingers over my temples again. My head was still pounding and I wasn't in the mood for any more of my uncle's bullshit games.

"Can you just give me a straight fucking answer already? I have a splitting headache and am not in the mood to play twenty questions to get the information you know I want."

He sighed like I was ruining his fun or something. Not that I gave a shit.

"Fine. You want the facts? Your father sold you and your mother to me the night before the fire."

My head jerked up so I could lock my gaze onto his. He couldn't have possibly said what I thought he had. Could he? "Sorry, he did what?"

I'd have loved to have been able to slap the slimy

smirk off his face, but was honestly too shocked by his revelation to even try.

"Yes, Grace. You see, my brother loved to gamble. He'd gotten addicted to the rush of it all, but unfortunately, he never was any good at it. In the end, he owed quite a substantial amount to a loan shark who had threatened to start breaking body parts if he didn't pay up. When he came to me to bail him out, I made it clear I couldn't simply gift him the funds. He needed to offer something in exchange. Sadly for him, by then all he had that was worth anything was you and your mother. It didn't take me long to convince him his only option was to sell you both to me. I was actually surprised at how easily he agreed to it. He was meant to deliver you both to me the afternoon of the fire. But instead of simply bringing you both to me, the fool tried to explain to your mother what he'd done, how it made sense. Naturally, she refused to come quietly. Gordon had thought he had her cowed enough to do anything he told her to, but turns out he didn't have her under his thumb as much as he'd thought. It was for you she fought. To protect her only daughter, she found her long forgotten spine and attacked him. Of course, he was stronger, and well, you know how that ended. Gordon fled after the fire got out of hand. He came to me begging for help. Again." He paused to take another drink. "Such a fool. I had my men take him to the police to be dealt with."

Bile churned in my stomach. Gordon had died way too quickly. He'd sold his wife and only daughter into human trafficking to pay a fucking gambling debt. What sort of man does that?

"What were you planning on doing with us?"

I almost didn't want to know what he'd planned, but the fact he'd come for me now had me thinking it was about to become my future, and I preferred to know rather than go into whatever it was blind.

Another of his shark smiles that had my skin feeling too small for my body didn't exactly ease my fears.

"Well, you'll be happy to know I had planned on allowing your mother to continue raising you." He paused a moment, like he was expecting me to thank him or some shit. When I stayed silent, he huffed before continuing. "Not full time, of course, only when she wasn't busy working in my stable. Gordon was a fool to keep a woman like her to himself. The money he could have made would have more than covered his debts if he'd been putting her to work since the beginning."

Bile rose up my throat, but I managed to swallow it down, while also refusing to let the tears that stung my eyes fall. My uncle had intended on pimping my mother out. My father, her husband, had *knowingly* sold her into sex slavery.

"Don't be so upset, my dear. You weren't ever going to end up there with her. You were much too valuable to waste like that. A sweet, innocent young girl who was already showing signs of the beauty she would grow up to be. You, I auctioned off. Made a large sum of money from that auction, and a powerful alliance with an up-and-coming Yakuza man."

I shook my head, what he said didn't add up. "Stop lying. How were you going to let my mother raise me, if you'd sold me off to some bloke in Japan? And what were you planning on doing with Donny? He never would have stopped looking for us."

Donny and I were half-siblings, with different fathers. Donny's dad had been the love of Mum's life. A US Marine who'd died in combat. He'd had a sister here in the US who Donny was sent to live with after the fire.

He frowned, "I have not lied. Kenjiro Takeda is not a pedophile, he wanted you for his wife. You were to be raised by your mother until you were eighteen. With your red hair, you're quite the novelty to Asians, and he wanted to ensure his future bride would be a virgin, who had been raised to know how to behave as a made-man's wife should. As for Donny, I would have brought him into the fold, made him a soldier for the family. He was still a teen, the perfect age to being training as an enforcer for the family."

I scoffed, he knew nothing about what type of man my brother was, but I wasn't going to correct him. Let him find out when Taz slit his throat for all he'd done.

"Well, considering it's been some time since my hymen was intact, and I was raised by an AFP agent to be the very opposite of what this fucker Kenjiro no doubt wants, I wouldn't have thought he'd be interested in me anymore. And are you trying to tell me he's what? Waited all these bloody years in the hopes I was still alive and would be found?"

Stupid tears of frustration stung my eyes again. My headache, that had finally begun to fade, stormed back to life at my uncle's continuing bullshit. He'd kidnapped me, was taking me far away from everyone who'd be able to help me, and now he was spinning some story that made no fucking sense.

He scoffed after draining the last of his whiskey. "Of course not. He has a wife and a daughter. That's why we're going to Hawaii. You're to be his mistress, hidden away from the world until you bare him a male heir he can train. Then he might divorce his wife to marry you. If you're lucky. Although, I doubt it if you continue to swear like you do. He'll want a lady. Oh, and the reason he still wants to take possession of you is because he paid a fuck ton of money to me for that privilege. I can't tell you how happy I am you survived that fire, my dear. Now my alliance with him and the Yakuza can get back on track and I can claim the power and position within the family I should have risen to over a decade ago."

Well, fuck. I was so screwed. Literally if I couldn't find a way to escape before this Kenjiro guy locked me away somewhere.

A young woman came toward us from the rear of the plane.

"Mr. Milani, are you ready for the dinner service?"

Trying to gage if she'd be an ally, I watched her closely as she sauntered up to stand beside my uncle before leaning down to pick up his empty glass from where he'd put it on the table between us. Obviously guessing my thoughts, my uncle held my gaze, and with a raised eyebrow, put his palm on her calf, sliding it up, taking her skirt with him as he stroked up the outside of her thigh.

Setting the glass back down, the woman straightened and with a moan of pleasure, shifted until she stood in front of him with her back to me. His gaze left me and went to her as he shoved the fabric of her skirt the rest of the way up, until it bunched around her waist, baring her lacy thong and stockings that were connected to garters.

"Very nice, pet. I hope your choice in underthings is an indicator of your skills."

I cringed at how breathy her voice had gone. "Yes, sir. I've been fully trained so am able to provide anything you require of me."

"Hmm. Tell me, pet, does your bra match these lovely knickers?"

"Yes, sir."

He gave her a sleazy smile he no doubt thought was sexy but made me want to puke. "Not sure I believe you. I'm going to need you to prove it to me. Strip down to your underwear. You're to stay that way until we need to prepare to land. Understand?"

"Yes, sir."

She immediately started to unbutton her blouse. Shock that this chick would follow orders, given by a stranger, with such ease left me speechless while she quickly shed the rest of her clothes, then stepped into the aisle to drape them over a vacant seat before returning to stand in front of my uncle. And it turned out she had not lied earlier, because her large —fake—breasts were barely contained in a lacy black bra that indeed matched the rest of her underwear.

"Do a turn for me, pet. Show me that lush arse of yours that I just got a glimpse of."

With a swing to her hips, she turned so she was now facing me, her back to my uncle. The smug smile she gave me had me rolling my eyes. Stupid idiot thought she was winning something from me. She couldn't be more wrong, but if she wanted to be a mafia mile high club whore, that was her choice.

With a groan, my uncle grabbed her cheeks and gave each a squeeze before he released her.

"Hands on the table, pet."

Less than a heartbeat later, she'd leaned forward as he'd ordered and he began to spank her. Delivering hard slaps to her arse until the scent of her arousal filled the air, making me scrunch my nose up before I shook my head in disbelief over the way she was obviously enjoying being treated like a fucking sex object by a perfect stranger.

"Turn around and drop to your knees, pet. You have one more job to do before you can get on with the dinner service."

"Yes, sir." Again, without hesitation, she turned and

lowered down to her knees, her fingers on his fly before I could blink. Fuck, she was keen. Shifting in my seat, I focused out the window, not wanting to see my uncle's dick but unfortunately, it wasn't such an easy task to block out the slurping and gagging noises the woman made as my uncle fucked her mouth.

Once I heard him close his zipper, I glanced over to see that he wasn't done with her. Still on her knees in front of him, he'd shoved her bra down and was toying with her breasts.

"Your surgeon did a marvelous job, pet. And the nipple rings are a nice touch."

"Thank you, sir. I'm glad you like them."

Probably a good thing I hadn't eaten yet. I was sure I'd have thrown it up by now if I had.

"After you bring us our dinner, you'll go to the cockpit dressed exactly like this and tell Ramirez that you are a gift to him from me to enjoy for his assistance today. His co-pilot can handle the plane while he enjoys you."

Her body stiffened a little when he'd mentioned Ramirez. Interesting. Guess she either knew him and didn't like him, or she just wasn't as eager to fuck the help, only a made-man. Either way, she was back smiling by the time she'd risen to her feet and turned toward the rear of the plane.

I reached out and grabbed her wrist as she passed. Pausing a few moments before I spoke to enjoy the way my uncle stiffened and lost his post-sex glow as he wondered what I was going to say.

"Could you please bring me some pain killers with dinner? I have a wicked headache."

She smiled, relief in her gaze. Apparently, like my uncle, she'd thought I was going to ask something less innocent. "Of course, ma'am. I'll get that sorted out for you and be back soon."

Once I released her wrist, she strode away and I turned back to glare at my uncle.

"Was that really necessary? Seriously? Getting the stewardess to blow you?"

"That was your fault, Grace. I had to prove to you that she would not help you in whatever scheme you were cooking up in that pretty head of yours. And once Ramirez finishes with her, our pilot will be more than happy to do anything I ask of him."

While I'd never before wished for unconsciousness, I was now. Because if I was out cold, I wouldn't have to hear any of the bullshit these men intended to inflict on the oh so willing stewardess.

"How much longer until we land?"

Throwing his head back he laughed at my obvious discomfort, but didn't offer up a fucking answer.

Bastard.

Chapter 19

Trident

By the time I got out to my bike, my cell was pinging with messages but I waited until after I'd reattached my saddle bag and started my bike before I checked them.

I was happy to see one was from Keys. I found myself actually holding my damn breath, hoping Jacie hadn't been flown too far away, as I opened it up.

> Private plane, flight path to Lihue, Kauai,
> Private unavailable for us. Fastest
> commercial flight leaves in an hour.
> American Airlines. Have told Viper.

He must have texted Viper before me, because the next message was from my president.

> Go to usual meet point near airport.
> Crew will meet you there. Tickets being
> sent to phones.

Sure enough, the next message was my airfare.

Fuck, it was going to be tough to get through to the gate in time with only an hour. Roaring away from the hotel, I weaved between traffic to get out to the industrial zone near the airport in record time, pulling into the parking lot of a SCMC owned factory moments before Maverick rolled in with a club cage following behind him. Viper must have sent them out the door the moment I'd texted him earlier.

Grabbing my saddle bag, I headed over to the vehicle. Maverick joined me as I popped the trunk and we both put our helmets and bags in. I also stripped off all my weapons and anything else I thought the TSA might take objection to.

"Me and Grinder will be joining you, Rubble's gonna drop us off to make shit faster."

We'd both rushed to disarm, and didn't slow until we were both sitting in the rear seat. Almost before we'd shut the doors, Rubble was pulling out and racing toward the airport. Maverick handed me one of the two backpacks that were on the seat between us. "For your cut, and the girls also packed some snacks and other shit for our trip in them."

Following Maverick and Grinder's lead, I shrugged out of my cut as we drove. After folding it carefully, I put it in the bag and zipped it up. I hated having to go without wearing my club colors, but there were times it was necessary.

"Maverick, you heard anything about Animal's condition?"

Our club VP looked over at me with a grim look. "He's still in surgery. Stone's staying close. Once he gets out, and wakes the fuck up, he'll have to answer for his actions this morning."

I grunted in response, because what else was there to say? Animal had fucked up royally, and there would be a price he'd need to pay for that. The most likely outcome was death, which meant those surgeons were wasting their fucking time fixing him up, but we could hardly go in there and tell them that.

Rubble parked right in front of the entrance we needed and in seconds all three of us were out and rushing toward the automatic doors. Felt strange as fuck without my colors on my back, but TSA would be a bitch if we went in wearing them, not to mention we weren't going into Hawai'i with permission from any of the local clubs, so it was safer to go in as civilians.

Thankfully, the security line was short and we got through to our gate in time to board. It was only once we were seated on the plane that I got a good look at our tickets. Fuck, ten hours and twenty minutes until we'd get there, with a half hour layover in Phoenix. Scrubbing a hand over my face, I mumbled a curse.

"What's wrong, brother?"

I looked at Grinder, who sat on my right. Maverick was on my left, in the window seat.

"I hate how long it's gonna take us to get there. She's on a private fucking jet that'll be flying direct."

He nodded, his expression grim. "I hear ya, but it is what it is. We were lucky to get on this flight. Viper checked other choices before going with Keys' recommendation. Every other option had much longer layovers."

"Yeah, I know, brother. I just want her fucking back and safe already."

Staring out the window as we took off, I couldn't avoid thinking about the fact I was going home for the first time in over two decades.

"You messaged Toa yet? Think he'll be able to help at all?"

I shook my head at Maverick's question. "Didn't have time. I'll give him a call while we're in Phoenix."

I'd barely spoken to my childhood friend since we'd left the USMC. While I'd stayed on the mainland, he'd gone back home to Kaua'i. The few texts we'd send each other on holidays or birthdays each year had never included much about our lives. So, I had no fucking clue if he was going to be able to help us beyond maybe a pick up from the airport. But I'd already planned on checking in with him before Maverick mentioned it.

Trying to get comfortable, I stretched my legs out as much as I could and rested my head against the seat. Closing my eyes, I was swamped with thoughts of the past, my parents. Which in turn brought on the usual guilt that always came whenever I went down memory lane.

I'd been two months off turning eighteen when my class had gone on a field trip to O'ahu, to tour Pearl Harbor. About ten minutes in, I'd known what I wanted to do with my life. Working for a bigger purpose than myself, helping to keep innocents safe, America safe, seemed like a noble quest to devote my life to. Having spent my entire childhood and teen years on or around the ocean, I'd figured the Navy was the way to go, but Toa, who'd been my best friend since we were toddlers, was hellbent on going into the USMC. He'd been so adamant that the Marines was where we needed to be, I'd been happy to follow his lead.

We'd both come home from that trip and told our parents, with paperwork in hand together with all the enthusiasm a teenager could have for a new idea. While Toa's parents voiced their worry for his safety, they were supportive and proud of their youngest son's decision. Mine, unfortunately, did not follow their example. My mother turned the drama on. Throwing her hands into the air and looking to the sky while questioning why the Gods would want to take her only son from her to die fighting some other man's war on the other side of the world.

I hadn't let her theatrics deter me. She'd always

been an extremely passionate woman who'd often reacted to the smallest of things with way more emotion than they warranted. Once I turned eighteen, I could sign all the paperwork and forms myself so it wasn't like I had to waste time changing her mind.

What I hadn't expected was my father backing my mother to the point he threatened to cut me from the family if I went through with enlisting. That had thrown me for a six. While my father would often give into my mother's whims in the moment, he would coax her into being realistic about it later.

He'd always been a big believer in the old ways, teaching me all about the legends and history of the Hawaiian people. He fished every day the weather permitted, selling his catch at the local markets, while my mother kept the house and tended the garden, growing all manner of things that would be sold at the markets along with the fish. Neither had ever left Kaua'i, not even to go to the Big Island, so I got they couldn't understand my desire to see the world.

I blew out a breath, wishing I could just go to fucking sleep instead of reliving all this shit. But now I'd started on this path down memory lane, I couldn't seem to turn it off. Memories of how I'd ignored their threats and continued to enlist. How I'd assumed they'd come around, be fucking proud of me. And how damn wrong I'd been.

When it was time to ship out, *Makua* had refused to take me to the airport, telling me he would not help me go to die halfway around the world in some desert I had no business being in. I'd gotten so mad. Said things I shouldn't have. Called him a coward, told him our warrior ancestors he'd taught me so much about would be disgusted with how he was treating me. Māmā had started crying like she'd just been sentenced to the gallows and between that and my words, *Makua* had lost his shit. It was the only time I'd ever seen him completely lose his temper. Only time he'd ever thrown a punch my way too.

My heart ached as I recalled walking away from them that day. Having to hitchhike my fucking way to the airport to meet up with Toa. Both of us being awkward as hell as we ignored my bruised eye and cheek even though he had to have guessed how I'd gotten it, while we waited to board our flight for San Diego to start basic training, at Parris Island. That had been the last time I'd seen or spoken to either of my parents. They'd written to me several times over the following couple of years, but I never opened them. I'd had enough to deal with on deployments without adding my mother's drama into the mix.

An announcement warning we were coming in to land in Phoenix pulled me back to the present and I switched my focus to potential plans on how I was going to first locate, then rescue my woman.

Turning to Maverick, I caught his attention. "You got Keys' number?"

"Yeah, why?"

With only half hour between our flights, we wouldn't have long to get shit done before we needed to board.

"While we're making our way to the next gate, can you check in with him for an update while I see if I can get hold of Toa?"

He nodded, "I was thinking along the same lines. Grinder, you call Viper, see what news he has for us."

The second the seatbelt sign dinged off, we were up and moving, making sure we were among the first to get off the plane. We had shit to do and plans to make.

Hold on, Ula'ula Mõ'ī, I'm coming for you.

Chapter 20

Jacie

As much as I didn't want to be handed over to some Yakuza bastard, I couldn't wait to get off this fucking plane. My uncle had taken great joy in using the stewardess to make me as uncomfortable as possible. I'd have felt sorry for her, but she'd appeared to honestly enjoy the attention; snuggling up to my uncle or disappearing with the pilot every chance she got.

At least my headache had eased after I'd eaten and taken some meds.

When she came sauntering down from the cockpit toward us, I couldn't hold back the sigh. Having to watch another round would surely have me throwing up the little I'd managed to eat.

She stopped next to my uncle's seat and before she could utter a word, he'd thrust one hand between her thighs and used the other to tug on one of her nipple rings. Her voice, now breathy as she stuttered her way through what she came to tell him. "The pilot, ah, would like you to know, hmmm, that we're about to start our decent into Lihu'e." She paused to moan, "Did you need anything before I get things put away, in preparation for landing?"

Uncle Terrence smirked my way as he continued to play with her. "I think we can get another orgasm or two outta you before then, don't you think, pet?"

She gripped the top of his seat with one hand as she lifted her leg, placing her foot on the seat between his legs and giving him one helluva view of all her pink bits.

"Hmm, such a good girl."

I gagged, on the verge of throwing up.

"I'm heading to the bathroom."

His laughter mixed in with the wet suction sounds of him finger fucking the chick followed me as I raced to the rear of the plane and shut myself into the small room. Leaning over the toilet, I mostly dry retched until sweat slicked my face. Dizzy, probably due to being at least slightly concussed thanks to Animal, I struggled to my feet and turned to the hand basin. After washing my hands and rinsing out my mouth, I cupped water in my palms to splash over my face, grabbing some paper towels to dry off.

Gripping the sides of the sink I stared at my pale face in the mirror.

"How the hell am I gonna get out of this one?"

Opening drawers, I found a disposable toothbrush kit and used it, taking my time so hopefully my uncle was finished before I had to go back out there. The attendant's voice accompanied a tap on the door.

"Ma'am? You need to return to your seat now."

"Be out in a sec!"

Tossing the toothbrush into the trash, I unlocked the door and made my way back to my chair, trying to ignore the way my uncle was smirking.

"You are adorably naive, Grace. Kenjiro will enjoy breaking you of that trait."

I clenched my jaw, refusing to take the bait as I looked out at the green island we were closing in on.

"Silent treatment? Really? I wouldn't have thought you'd be so childish, but at least it means you're not swearing so I won't force you to answer me."

Bastard liked the sound of his own voice way too much. The stewardess returned from the rear area now fully dressed and moved to the front where she strapped herself into a seat near the cockpit. I mentally shook my head at how put together she appeared. No one would ever guess she'd basically been the star of an orgy for the past several hours.

Blowing out a breath I turned back to the window, watching the little airport get bigger and bigger. I'd always wanted to visit Hawaii, but not like this. And certainly not to live here forever. Tears stung my eyes at the thought of never seeing Taz, Flick or Lolly again. Of never meeting the new baby. Blinking faster, my heart nearly cracked open when Trident's face filled my thoughts. He was so bloody perfect for me. Strong enough to stand up to me, his sense of humor was twisted enough he enjoyed bantering with me. He could command my body like no man ever had before. All he'd wanted was to show the world I was his and instead of accepting it with some grace, I went crazy bitch on him.

Thankfully, before I could go too far down that rabbit hole, the plane landed with a small bump, then slowed before taxiing toward an open hanger. Naturally, we weren't going to the public terminal where I may have been able to catch the attention of security. Not that I'd honestly expected for that to be an option, not with how my luck was going.

Once the plane had stopped and all the checks and shit had been done, and the outside door had been opened. A pair of armed men of Asian appearance entered and stood near the exit, on full alert. Uncle

Terrence unclipped his seatbelt and stood, holding a hand to me.

"Come, Grace, it's time to meet your new master."

Fuck me, and I'd complained about Trident wanting to make me his property. At least he hadn't wanted the title of being my master. No one would ever be my fucking owner. I wasn't a fucking pet.

Knowing that I needed to bide my time, to play passive until Kenjiro or his men underestimated me—which would give me the best chance of successfully escaping—didn't make it any easier to actually do it. Grinding my teeth, I undid my seat belt and put my hand in his, hating that I was being forced to touch him. Especially when I knew where his hands had been recently.

He pulled me up with a tug that sent me slamming against his body.

"Did you not enjoy the in-flight entertainment, my dear?"

Glaring, I spoke quietly, so only he'd hear. "You will pay with your fucking life for what you've done. Mark my words."

With a broad grin, teeth flashing, he laughed before moving my hand to the crook of his arm and leading me toward the exit. He stopped near the goons and turned away from me to open a cupboard. Frowning, I wondered what the hell he was doing. When he returned to me, the last thing I expected to see him holding was my handbag. Thanks to Animal lying about my phone, it was hopefully still in there. Refusing to give away how excited I was to have it back, I waited until he held it out to me before I lifted my hand to take it.

"In case we get stopped by airport security, you'll need your ID. It will also help to keep our driver oblivious to the situation." He frowned. "He is from a local service and not in the employ of Kenjiro. If you try to get him to aid you in any way, it'll mean his death, and harsh punishment for you that'll take considerable time for you to recover from. Do I make myself clear?"

Once more, I clenched my teeth so I didn't verbally lash out in front of the armed guards and show them how much of a fighter I really was. I merely nodded as I slung my handbag over my shoulder. At the bottom of the stairs, I opened my bag and checked my phone was still in there while I pulled out a lip balm, applying it to my dry lips before tossing it back in and making sure it was firmly closed. Uncle Terrance scowled my way.

"What? I didn't drink enough water on the flight, my lips are chapped."

He shook his head before marching over to the large black SUV. It took effort to not roll my eyes at the luxury Cadillac Escalade that was about the furthest thing anyone would think when they thought of Hawaii. Guess all mobsters were alike in some ways.

Keeping silent as I watched the absolute gorgeous scenery pass by, I mentally took note of every turn and town name. If I could get free, I'd need to be able to return to the airport to get back to the mainland. When I'd told my uncle earlier that I'd been raised by an AFP agent to be everything he wouldn't want me to have become, he seemed to think I was just throwing out bullshit, but I wasn't. My adoptive father had taught me a lot, on top of what I learned in my training with the Australian Federal Police. I'd also taken martial arts my entire life, and had discovered early I had a natural talent with languages and could speak five fluently. I had a feeling the fact Japanese was one of them was going to come in rather handy.

When we finally pulled into a long drive, my jaw

dropped at how pretty it was. Sure, it was big and fancy, but with the cream walls, brown timber accents and roof tiles, it was absolutely stunning. The lush green, perfectly manicured gardens, added to the opulent feel of the place. I cursed under my breath when we pulled up under a drive-through-carport area, like one you'd see at a boutique hotel. Not waiting for one of the goons to open my door, I let myself out and didn't have to fake my awe as I took in everything. Uncle Terrence chuckled, clearly amused at my wonder, which I was only hamming up slightly so I could take a few extra moments to catalog what was around the house. Lots of the plants were big and bushy, good for hiding behind. But the two roaming guards were an issue. There was no way to know if they did their patrols twenty-four/seven. Hopefully they only walked the yard during the day, and just guarded the doors at night. I could work with that.

"C'mon, Grace, let's get you settled inside. Kenjiro will be here shortly, and he wants you showered and dressed appropriately for what he has planned."

I could just imagine what 'appropriate' meant in Kenjiro's mind. Since none of the men were currently focused on me, I rolled my eyes at my uncle before I turned toward him.

"Yeah, whatever."

As I slowly made my way toward the front door, I let my gaze track the leaving SUV, using it as an excuse to take in more of the grounds; noting the distance to the road, how far away the neighboring houses were. I was confident if I could find a way to sneak out of the house undetected during the night, I would be able to escape.

Stepping through the door when one of the guards held it open for us, I paused in shock.

"Whoa."

"Shoes off, pet."

Without taking my gaze off the view, I slipped my feet out of my sandals. While my adoptive parents had been well off, and I'd never wanted for anything I truly needed, I'd never been in such an opulent house before. Without thought, I moved forward, around the two plush white couches and fancy solid looking coffee table, stopping before I went out through the open bi-fold patio doors. The sight that greeted me was like a postcard come to life. A crystal-clear pool, surrounded with comfortable looking loungers and large umbrella shades and beyond that was a vista of paradise. Mountains rose up on the other side of the small bay that was near the house, the water was blue, the sand white. Under any other circumstances, I'd have loved the chance to stay here.

Uncle Terrence wrapped his hand around my elbow and pulled me toward the northern wing of the house. "You've got the rest of your life to stand there staring at the view, right now you need to go freshen up and change before the others arrive."

Easily keeping pace with him, I frowned. "Others?"

He nodded absently. "You'll find out soon enough. Right, this is your room. Private bathroom and walk in robe" he pointed as he spoke "You'll find both stocked with everything you need. Change into the outfit left on the bed, nothing other than what is there. Understand? You don't need shoes. You have about half an hour. If you're not ready, I'll drag you out there naked. No skin off my nose."

Thrusting me into the room, I spun to glare at him. "Do you feel no familial ties to me? A little concern over what's going to happen to me?"

That shark smile of his made another appearance. "I'm well aware that we share a blood tie. After all, that was the reason selling you benefited me so much." He moved to close the door but paused. "Oh, all the windows and exterior doors are locked and alarmed. Don't bother wasting your time trying to escape, even if you did make it outside, the roaming guards would pick you up in seconds."

The snick of the lock after he closed me in had fury filling me, until I had to vent some of it. With a scream, I tossed my handbag onto the bed. When it landed with a thud, I winced at how stupid my outburst had been. My phone was the only lifeline I had left and I needed to be more careful with it. As I was about to reach for my bag, Trident's deep gravelly voice filled my mind, saying how important it was to always thoroughly check any new area you found yourself in before lowering your guard. I quickly looked through each part of my prison. Shaking my head when I discovered that while the walk-in robe was filled with clothes my size, there were no shoes. No doubt my sandals had vanished from beside the front door too. Did they honestly think that would stop me from trying to leave? I'd walk barefoot over broken glass to be free of these people.

With a sigh, I grabbed the clothing that had been left for me to wear. A simple sleeveless dress in a stunning Hawaiian themed fabric; white with large blue flowers. The top part was stretchy and would hug my chest snuggly, and left me praying it would be tight enough to stay up considering it wasn't like I had huge boobs to anchor it. I cringed at the lacy G-string and strapless bra that was way racier than anything I'd pick to wear myself.

"Well, chick. This is life for now."

Grabbing my handbag, I went into the bathroom, tossing the outfit onto the counter before going to lock the door. I hadn't seen any cameras, but those fuckers could be super small and I couldn't be one-hundred percent sure I hadn't missed finding them. Leaning against the door, I reached into my bag for my phone, powering it on. As I waited for it to load up, I pondered over who I should contact. Strangely, it was Trident that came to mind first. Probably because I'd just been thinking about him as I'd searched. Taz was the more logical choice, or Keys who ran Athena Security for the club. The moment the screen lit up, I fumbled to get it on silent as it started to ping with a bunch of missed calls and texts.

"Whoa, well, okay then."

There were dozens of messages and calls from various people. Including one from my adoptive father, a request to call him urgently. Guess he got wind of Uncle Terrence's plan just a fraction too late. Warmth filled my chest when I saw the last message was from Trident.

I will find you, Ula'ula Mŏ'ī. Hold on.

Leaning my head back against the door, I squeezed my eyes closed as tears leaked down my cheeks. I loved him. It was completely insane. We'd only known each other for such a short time, but there was no denying he was already a part of my heart and soul.

Dashing my tears away, I forced myself to focus on the present. I'd witnessed firsthand how fast an MC could get shit done. They had a huge advantage of not having to follow a bunch of rules or worry about red tape like my father would have to because he worked with the AFP. It was an easy decision in the end to trust the Satan's Cowboys and Charon MCs with rescuing me. I quickly set up a text to Taz, Trident and Keys' phone numbers.

Taken by Terrance Milani. Sold to Kenjiro
Takeda. In Princeville Kauai. Unsure how
many guards.

That should cover the basics. Once Keys got my message, he'd know my phone was on and track it to pinpoint my exact location. When Trident got it, he'd know what direction to come while he waited for Keys to give him more information. Returning my phone to my bag, I set it on the bench near the sink, then went and turned the insanely big shower on. As I stood under the warm water, Trident's nickname for me played through my mind. He'd said it was Hawaiian, and he did have the tanned complexion that fit with him having a Hawaiian heritage. What were the chances he was from this island though? That he'd have support here to help him rescue me.

Chapter 21

Trident

As much as I wanted to get out of the airport and start searching for Jacie as fast as possible, I was nervous as hell about the greeting I was in for.

Grinder was looking around with wide eyes and shook his head when we came off the plane and into the interior of the small airport.

"Fuckin' open air terminal. For real. Wouldn't believe this shit if I wasn't seeing it."

I looked around, taking in the two luggage carousels on either side of the large open space. While there was a roof over this area, there were only half-walls and planter boxes to separate it from the outside. Not much had changed in the last couple of decades, other than the expected TSA and tech additions. Although I hadn't expected anything different, things on Kaua'i ran at a slower, more relaxed pace. My city born and bred brothers would be in for quite the culture shock.

"Is there seriously a fuckin' rooster walking through here like he owns the damn place?"

Grinning I watched the little guy strut his way across the floor before hopping up into a raised garden bed.

"Yeah, those little suckers are everywhere across the island. *Aloha, braddah.* It's been a minute. We gotta catch up in person more often than every twenty fucking years, yeah?"

Noa 'Toa' Wailani was a big man. At six foot five he towered over my six two. He had broad shoulders and the solid build of a traditional Hawaiian warrior. He'd always looked that way, and had earned the nickname Toa, Hawaiian for warrior, before we hit the USMC. His black hair was cropped short and it looked like he hadn't shaved for a day or two. He wore a tank under his colors, showing off the full sleeves of Hawaiian themed ink that covered his arms down to his wrists. Those were new since I'd last seen him, but then, I had more than a touch of ink he didn't know about. I was shocked to see the patch on his cut declaring he was the president of his club. We really did need to talk more often.

I stretched a hand toward him, unsure if he'd want to greet me as we'd used to. He took my hand and shook it, as he reached with his other arm to pull me in a Hawaiian *'greet with breath'* greeting. Resting a palm on the back of my neck and his forehead against mine, I closed my eyes while gripping the back of his neck in return. Fuck, I'd missed him.

"Damn, it's good to see you. Wish it was under better circumstances, but I'll take what I can get."

He turned to my club brothers and I introduced them.

"Maverick, our club VP and Grinder, club secretary."

He gave each man a nod in greeting as I'd said their names.

"Welcome to Kaua'i, braddahs. I'm Toa, president of the Losi Kahu MC. I've known Trident since we were both in diapers, served with him in the USMC. His pain is mine and I have my club ready to help in any way we can to rescue his woman."

Maverick responded before I could. "Appreciate it. What transport do you have for us?"

He tilted his head toward the exit. "I brought a cage to take you back to our clubhouse. We waiting on any luggage?"

Shaking my head, I started moving. "Nope, we didn't check anything. Let's get outta here."

It didn't take long for us to cross over to the parking lot and load up in the Ford Explorer Toa had brought. As we sped down the road my phone dinged with a message, my whole being going on alert when I saw who it was from.

"Got a message from her, *brahs*"

Maverick leaned forward from where he sat in the rear seat. "What's it say?"

"She's here, in Princeville. Confirms it was her uncle that took her... " I couldn't speak through my rage at what I read next. My whole body tensed, ready to throw cracks on someone, but with no available target, I ended up tightening my grip on my phone so much the thing creaked. When a fissure spread across the top corner of the screen, I dropped the phone to my lap, shoving my hands into my hair and tugging at my braids, trying to calm down enough that I could fucking function.

Maverick snatched my phone and was soon growling his own anger. "Mother-fucking-bastard sold her. That fucker is gonna die hard. Fucking selling his niece. Toa, you ever heard of someone called Kenjiro Takeda?"

When he didn't answer Maverick immediately, I

glanced his way to see he was maybe as furious as I was; his knuckles white with how tight he was gripping the steering wheel, his muscles along his jaw twitching as he ground his teeth.

Forcing my way back to sanity for my friend, I laid a palm on his shoulder.

"Toa? You with me, *braddah?*"

Hissing out a breath, he tilted his head side to side, cracking his neck before he loosened his hold on the steering wheel and spoke. "Yeah, I know the fucka. He's Japanese, Yakuza. Wasn't sure he still had a place here."

It was easy to pick up there was a whole lot Toa wasn't saying, but before I could ask him to elaborate, my phone dinged with another text.

Maverick's tone had a dash of admiration in it when he spoke. "It's from Keys, giving us a location. Damn, Trident, your girl is something else. Not only did she find a way to keep her fucking phone, but she's managed to use it without getting caught."

A chill ran down my spine as Maverick handed me back my phone. "We don't know that. That she wasn't caught."

I didn't want to think about what a Yakuza man would do to a woman who defied him.

Maverick gripped my shoulder, squeezing it. "No way would Jacie get caught. I've read what we have on her. Her adopted dad was Australian Federal Police, and she went into the same field. Sure, she works for Athena Security now, but that woman's got a whole lot of training. She ain't gonna make dumb mistakes."

With a deep breath, I nodded. He was right. Jacie was intelligent and careful.

"Fuck. Okay. Yeah. Right. And she was clever enough to know who to fucking message to get her rescued. She knew I'd be coming for her, knew Keys would be the fastest to pinpoint her location. She probably also messaged Taz. Toa, you should expect some more bikers coming in. Her brother is with the Charon MC, one of our support clubs. They're good guys."

"I'll let my *braddahs* know. Give them my number, tell them to keep me updated on any arrivals so we can get them taken care of."

Looking at the message, I read the location. Princeville was up on the north coast of the island, and we'd taken off in that direction when we'd left the airport.

"Toa, where's your clubhouse? And how far from it is Princeville?"

"We're about ten minutes out from the clubhouse, and normally it'd take about half an hour to get to Princeville from there, but you know damn well we can do it a lot quicker when we need to."

He looked my way for a moment, and I gave him a hard stare. "We need to. She was flown in on a private plane, no layovers. He's already had her way too long."

While even five minutes was too fucking long as far as I was concerned, the fact he'd had hours with her had my gut churning. Toa nodded, then focused back on the road, he put his foot down, speeding up as we headed further north up the coast. Flipping back into the text from Jacie, I paused before I sent her a response. I didn't want to say too much in case someone other than her got hold of her phone, but I wanted to let her know we were close and coming for her.

C U soon

Staring at the screen, I contemplated writing more. Telling her how she was my fucking world and I needed her to hold on, stay strong. But in the end, decided against it and hit send. She was a fucking warrior woman, I didn't need to tell her to fight. And I'd tell her everything else when I had her back in my arms where she damn well belonged.

Before pocketing my phone, I sent a text to Keys, giving him Toa's number in case they were sending a crew. I also let him know we'd be at Jacie's location within the hour.

It was only a few minutes later when the car slowed to pull into a dirt drive at the foot of a mountain. From the street, the place didn't look like much. In fact, if you didn't know where to turn, you'd miss it. Once we got past the roadside shrubbery, there were a few buildings scattered around a property that was surrounded by heavy bushland on two sides.

"Nice set up."

Toa nodded. "It's served us well. We have dirt bike tracks all over the mountain too. After we get your woman back, I'll take you and your boys out for a ride. Be like old times, yeah?"

I had to grin at the reminder. From a young age, Toa and I had had dirt bikes, spending our weekends testing our skills and exploring the island.

"That'd be great."

Parking the car, we grew serious as we exited and he led us over to the biggest of the buildings.

"Welcome to the Losi Kahu MC clubhouse. I'll have one of the braddahs show you to a couple of rooms you can use while you're here. While you dump your stuff and get your cuts on, I'll get a crew and supplies together. We should be back on the road in under ten minutes. Thinking it'll be best if we take cars, bikes will be too fucking loud. They'll hear us coming long before we get there."

As much as we'd be faster if we took bikes, I had to agree with him. The other reason for taking a cage, that none of us wanted to give voice to, was that we didn't know what condition Jacie would be in when we found her.

True to his word, it was less than ten minutes later that we were heading out the door. Maverick, Grinder and I, along with Toa headed back to the Ford Explorer while six more Losi Kahu braddahs piled into the two Jeeps that had been brought up from a garage further back on the property while we'd been sorting shit out inside. We were now all fully armed for a battle, but there were no guns. The plan was for stealth; to get in and out without gaining attention from anyone outside of Takeda's property. That meant a whole lot of knives. Although, Toa had also grabbed a hatchet, while one of his brothers, Mene, had taken both a full sized and mini crossbow. The young guys had grabbed hunting knives and Tasers, which had Toa shaking his head.

It was utterly insane. But it was also fucking perfect.

Maverick and Grinder had shaken their heads when they looked over all the options. Most of the time, the SCMC went in with guns blazing when we had business to take care of. But I rather loved that Toa had put the effort in to having so many traditional, old school weapons for his crew to use. Many looked to be hand crafted from locally grown timber and tiger shark teeth.

I'd grabbed several modern throwing knives, along with a Pàhoa, a wooden bladed weapon with razor sharp shark teeth all down the curved edge. Swiping it across both Milani's and Takeda's throats was something I was looking forward to doing very soon. I'd also slipped what was essentially a set of knuckle dusters, but made from timber with more shark teeth attached across the top edge. It would cause a helluva lot of damage whether I slashed it or cracked with it. The weapons were brutal and primal, and worthy of what we were heading to do: rescue of an innocent; one of our family.

As we'd discussed earlier, all three cars pulled off the road about a quarter of a mile from the property. We quickly piled out, and three of the younger Losi Kahu braddahs moved to the driver seats to move the vehicles further away until they got word to come in, while the remaining six of us took off down the road. All the trees and shit made it easy to stay hidden as we worked our way quickly up the street. I had a throwing knife in my hand ready and Mene, one of the local crew had his crossbow loaded and ready to shoot.

Jogging beside Toa felt right, like old times and how it was meant to be. As much as I loved my SCMC brothers, I hadn't grown up with them, hadn't gone through USMC bootcamp and deployments by their sides. Toa was the closest thing I'd ever had to a blood brother, and I hadn't fully realized how much I'd missed him until now.

Mene had led the way, and as we got near the property line, he stopped to lift and aim his crossbow. He fired two arrows, both landing with quiet thunks. He must have shot true, as the men made no sound other than the thud of their bodies falling. We jogged up the drive but didn't stop at the front door. One of the other Losi Kahu took off to the left, while Mene, after he'd slung the larger weapon over his back and grabbed his smaller one, had moved further ahead of us and away from the house to the right. Their jobs were to clear the grounds of all outside guards, call an all clear to the drivers to bring the vehicles in, then come back us up inside.

From what we'd been able to find online, the easiest place to gain entrance was through the rear of the house where there was a wide series of bi-fold doors between the outside pool and the inside living room. We hoped they were open as they'd been in the old realtor page we'd found. If not, Maverick had grabbed a glass cutter, while Grinder had a lock pick he was very good at using.

Unlike Mene, I stuck close to the house as I led my small team toward the back, shaking my head as I stepped over a dead man with an arrow in his eye. Reaching the end of the wall, I pressed up against the bricks before carefully looking around the corner, grateful for the palms and other plants along the rear wall that hid me from view. Not that there was anyone around to see me. Happy to see the doors were wide open, I signaled the others to follow me. Staying low, we silently moved over the tiles, keeping close to the plants as we approached the opening. The closer we got, the more we could hear of what was going on inside. Not that it helped, since they weren't speaking English. There was also a buzzing noise that stopped and started regularly. I paused and cocked my head to try to hear it better. I'd definitely heard it before, but for the life me, I couldn't identify it.

Grinder moved up beside me, speaking directly into my ear so the sound didn't travel.

"Tattoo machine."

Looking down at my feet for a moment, I ground my teeth in anger, and disbelief, because now that Grinder had suggested it, I knew he was right. Someone in that house was getting a fucking tattoo, and what's the bet it wasn't Milani or Takeda.

Raising my head, I looked first at Grinder and

Maverick, then Toa in the eye, seeing my own rage and agony reflected back at me from each of them. I mouthed the words, "They all die today."

All three nodded and tapped their fists over their hearts, in a silent vow. Then we got back to work, continuing with renewed determination to get inside and take these fuckas down.

Chapter 22

Jacie

After seeing the responses from Trident, Taz and Keys, I'd been feeling pretty confident I wouldn't be stuck here for long. I'd just finished brushing out my damp hair when my uncle came banging on my door as he unlocked it then came in.

"You better be ready, Grace. I will drag you out there if I need to." I set the brush down just as he appeared in the bathroom's doorway, "Dammit, why is your hair still wet? You really don't want to start off on the wrong foot with Kenjiro, Grace."

I glared fire his way. "You do realize that half an hour is not much time to get ready? Especially if you want someone with my amount of hair to wash and dry it."

He shook his head, dismissing the conversation. "At least you're wearing the dress left for you. C'mon, he's waiting."

Taking a deep breath, I straightened my shoulders and followed my uncle out of my room and down the hallway and out into the living room. Two men stood in front of the open doorway, looking out of the pool to the coastline beyond, with their hands clasped behind their backs.

"Kenjiro, as promised, I deliver Grace Milani to you."

As my uncle spoke, the two men turned to face us. One wore a suit and looked like the rich arsehole he no doubt was. It wasn't like nice folks went around buying people, right? The other wore suit pants but no jacket, he also had his sleeves rolled up over his arms, and a gun and knife attached to his belt. Clearly the muscle out of the pair, and most likely Kenjiro's personal bodyguard.

"And only eight years past due. Since you haven't fulfilled your side of our agreement completely. I don't need to either."

Uncle Terrence stepped away from me and closer to Kenjiro, shaking his head. "No, no, no. I have done all you asked. As soon as I discovered she was alive, I went to great trouble and expense to find her and bring her here to your home. I made sure she cleaned up and dressed in the outfit you dictated she should wear. What haven't I done?"

Tilting his head to the side, Kenjiro ran his gaze over me from head to foot, the coldness in him had a shiver run down my spine and before I could stop myself, I rubbed my palms over my arms before crossing them across my chest. He returned his stare to my uncle, as if I'd somehow just proved his point.

"You were meant to see to her training and protection as she matured. Clearly, she hasn't been taught anything I need her to know. I paid you for a virginal woman, trained in how to be the wife of a Yakuza leader, instead you abandoned her to become what you gift me with today. She can be nothing more than a *mekake* now."

Maybe being able to speak Japanese wasn't going to

be as helpful as I'd first thought. Call me a concubine, will he? My temper flared fast and hot, and forgetting that I was meant to be playing the demure little woman, I stormed past my uncle, dodging his attempts to grab me and went right up to the prick, yelling at him in his native tongue as I came to a stop.

"How dare you say I'm good for nothing but being your concubine! I'm an educated, independent woman; with a solid job where I earn a good wage. I have my own apartment and provide everything I need by myself, with my own bloody money. I sure as fuck don't need a man's permission to be more than a sex toy! I will never be owned by any man. Uncle Terrence had no right to sell me to you in the first place. I'm a human being and I won't ever be anyone's possession."

He didn't move through my entire tirade until I'd finished, then he simply smirked at me before he responded in English.

"You can speak Japanese, a boon I hadn't expected." He glanced up to my uncle, "A skill I'm sure she learned with no thanks to you."

That had me growling. "Of course it was no thanks to him! I taught myself. And you can't buy Grace Milani because she doesn't exist anymore. I'm Jacie Lewis, not the same girl."

That got me a raised eyebrow. "The name witness protection gave you makes no difference. You are still Grace Milani, the daughter of a gambling addict who sold his wife and child into slavery to be able to clear his debts so he could live another day to make another bet."

My hand moved lightning fast and cracked across his face before I could stop myself. I grinned at how his head had snapped to the side, before he raised his own palm to cover the red imprint of mine I'd left on his face. My joy was short-lived however, because before I could take a breath, his bodyguard was on me. Pulling my hands behind my back to hold them in one of his large palms while he wrapped the other around the front of my neck, squeezing hard enough to make it clear to me that I was at his mercy.

Dropping his hand down, Kenjiro looked me in the eye, his gaze cold as ice. "You'll pay for that. But not until after I mark you as mine. It is important, after all, to label your belongings, is it not?"

"For the love of all that is holy, Grace, shut the hell up!"

Uncle Terrence's voice was strained, as though I was a great embarrassment to him. The goon holding me loosened his grip when I turned my head to glare over my shoulder at him. "If you'd wanted a mouse, you should have left me where you found me. I'll never be that woman."

Kenjiro sighed. "Like I said. You did not hold up your end of our bargain, Milani. You need to pay for that."

Before I could work out his intent, he'd pulled a small throwing knife from inside his suit jacket and pitched it at my uncle.

"What the fuck?"

I would have jumped back but I was being held too tightly to move. My gaze stayed on my uncle as he reached for the knife embedded in his chest but stumbled and fell to the floor before he could do more than touch it. He coughed a few times then began wheezing. Great, the bastard had missed my uncle's heart so now we'd have to listen to him die slowly. I tried to force away the compassion that rose up inside me for how he was suffering. He was evil and didn't deserve any pity.

"You should be happy, no? Surely you can agree

that the world is a better place without a man who would buy and sell his own niece in it?"

I turned to glare at him. "I think you're a fucking hypocrite since you're the arsehole who bought me from him."

He moved to stand closer and as soon as the man holding me released my neck, Kenjiro backhanded me across the face hard enough my head slammed into the goon's chest.

"I am your master; your owner. The one who controls every moment of your life, every choice you make. Including how you speak. No more swearing or you'll feel the bite of my whip, not just my hand." He focused on his goon then. "Get her tied down and find something to gag her. Let's get this part done so we can move forward."

Focusing on glaring after Kenjiro as he moved toward the front door, I hadn't expected the goon to start walking and I stumbled trying to stay upright.

"Just do as he says. It'll be easier on everyone, including you."

"What exactly did he mean by tie me down?"

He laughed as he forced me closer to the coffee table I'd admired earlier for how solid and strong it had looked. "I think you're smart enough to work that one out all by yourself, girl."

Tugging at my hands, it was easy to ignore his girl insult as I put all my focus and effort into trying to break free of his grip. But nothing worked. Landing a kick to his shins just earned me a growl and a shake, then he was in the wrong position for me to headbutt him or try to kick him again.

Dammit. Where the hell was Trident?

Chapter 23

Trident

Checking my grip on my throwing knife, and that the ones in my belt were all ready for me to grab quickly, I rolled my shoulders then, getting back low, continued to move forward toward the doorway. Having checked that my crew were ready to follow me in, I stepped into the open with my arm raised; the knife leaving my fingers before the men inside could even register my presence. I'd aimed at the bastard who was standing over Jacie, tattoo machine in his hand. My woman had been lashed down with rope to a fucking coffee table and gagged. Fuck, she could be a handful, and I'd thought about tying her up a time or two, but never like this. Never so she could be branded like she was fucking cattle.

My aim was true and since the Japanese bastard had turned toward me as I'd expected him to do, my blade sunk straight into his chest; hitting his heart. He stumbled back a step before crashing to the ground. Two other guards came running up from the basement but I didn't need to worry, they'd barely made it into the room before one had an arrow through an eye. Mene was out there covering our backs like the legend he was. The other ended up with a hatchet embedded between his eyes. I was gonna have to talk to Toa later to ask where he'd picked up the ability to throw a damn axe that fucking far with enough force to do that sort of damage. But I wasn't gonna waste time on it now.

Maverick had gone for the man I assumed was Takeda, who'd been sitting on the couch beside the coffee table. He'd stood up when we'd stormed in and had tried to pull a knife, but Maverick had been on him, knocking it away, before he had the chance to do anything with it. Then taking him down to the ground and with his hands pinned against his lower back, sat on him. Clearly, my club's VP was going to allow me to deal with him when I was ready.

Grinder had gone over to Jacie and removed the gag from her mouth. There were tears streaming down her face, but I wasn't sure if they were from pain, fury or relief. I went toward them, scanning the room as I moved. Looked like her uncle had met his end before we'd gotten here. The knife in his lung was not one of ours. I paused beside Maverick and Kenjiro.

"Get him on his feet, brother."

In seconds, I was staring into the eyes of a monster. Even now he was calm, too fucking calm. We'd just killed all his crew, and he had to know he was next.

"I have plenty more guards who will be here any moment."

A heavy thump near the rear entrance had us both glancing that way. Mene stood there, having just dropped the body of one of his men, who naturally had an arrow through his fucking eye. I was gonna be seeing that wound in my damn dreams with how often I'd seen it today.

"You mean these guys? Afraid they're all dead. Guess you're alone. But no worries, you'll be joining 'em real soon. Right, Trident?"

I shook my head with a huff. Damn crazy bastard. Then focused back on Kenjiro, who was finally starting to look scared.

"You took my woman from me." He opened his mouth to speak but I didn't give him the chance to say anything. "Yeah, I know it was your buddy over there that took her, but it was on your fucking orders. And it was you sitting here watching my woman be tattooed against her fucking will just now."

"She's mine, she's been mine since she was a child, long before you even knew she existed. My claim trumps yours. And I was simply labeling my property just now."

Hearing this bastard put it like that, had me understanding Jacie's issue with being called property better. She was thinking like this fucker, not like a biker's old lady.

"Just kill the asshole already, Trident, so we can get outta here."

I gave Maverick a nod, then pulled out my *Pàhoa* and swiped it across the fucker's throat, Maverick spun him to the side before releasing him so the blood that spurted from his wound hit the floor not any of us.

Dropping the *Pàhoa*, I rushed over to the table, where Grinder had just finished cutting her free from all the ropes. Lifting her into my arms, I sat on the couch that Kenjiro hadn't been sitting on, and settled her sideways on my lap, holding her close against me. With a broken sob, she wrapped her arms tightly around my neck and buried her face against my chest.

"I got you, *Ula'ula Mõ'ī*. You're safe now."

Closing my eyes, I pressed a kiss to the top of her head.

"Fuck, babe. We can't do this again. You are my heart, I can't live without you. I fucking love you, Jacie. I don't care that it's only been a damn week. Us being together was written in the fucking stars. Meant to be."

Her grip tightened on me a moment before she shifted, lifting away from my chest to look up at me. It killed me to see the tears that were slipping down her cheeks. Moving my hands to cup her face, I ran my thumbs over the tracks, wiping them away, hating the redness over the right side that meant one of these fuckas had hit her.

Lowering, I pressed my lips to hers, kissing her softly, with care, before I rested my forehead against hers and just breathed her in. Taking her scent deep into my lungs.

"I love you too, Trident. So much. And you're right, time doesn't matter, neither does our age difference. Labels are irrelevant. As long as we're together, nothing else is important."

Unable to resist, I covered her mouth with mine again, kissing her deeply, ignoring the few tears that escaped and slipped down my cheek to soak into my beard. This woman was my *hale*; my home, and now, not only did I have her back safe in my arms, but she loved me; accepted my claim on her.

My heart was finally whole.

Chapter 24

Jacie

I'd clung to Trident, refusing to release him from the moment he picked me up off that table until he locked us inside a bathroom at the Losi Kahu MC clubhouse. Then I'd had no choice but to let go so we could both strip off. Once naked, Trident paused with a pained look on his face as he gently ran a fingertip over the hot mess of a tattoo Kenjiro's man had inked on me. His head bodyguard was no tattoo artist, that's for sure. He hadn't appeared to like the idea much more than I had. But when Kenjiro had returned from wherever the fuck he went while I was being tied down, he'd been holding all the gear needed to tattoo someone. When his goon had hesitated, Kenjiro had ordered him to ink his name on me, threatening that he would kill him if he didn't do it.

At least it was in Japanese characters so no one would know what it said. Although, everyone would see the damn thing because they'd inked it just under my collarbone. Unless I started wearing high-neck shirts all the time.

Once I got back to Bridgewater I'd corner Silk and talk to her about it. She was an amazing tattooist and owned her own shop, Silky Ink. I was sure she'd be able to work out a way to cover up the thing and make it look fabulous.

"Can't believe anyone would do this."

I shrugged a shoulder, not wanting him to focus on it right now. I'd cried a river of tears already and I didn't want to continue.

"Plenty of people get names tattooed on them, T. Nothing out of the ordinary really."

He narrowed his gaze at me for a few seconds before he obviously saw in my eyes that I was trying to push past it, then his expression cleared and he leaned in and kissed me gently again.

"Well, they're all fools. C'mon, *Ula'ula Mõ'ī*, let's get cleaned up and into bed. I wanna sleep all night with you wrapped in my arms, where I know you'll be safe."

Pressing my palms against his pecs, I rose up on my toes to kiss him again. "Sounds perfect."

Taking my hand in his, he led me over to the shower. Once he got the water sorted out, he stepped in and pulled me in against him. Holding me for a few moments before he reached for the soap and started methodically washing me while I traced the lines of his muscles, needing to keep touching him.

We didn't linger under the spray for long; he looked as tired as I felt. Once out, he toweled me off. Making my heart melt with how gentle he was being, so unlike his usual rough, gruff biker way. This sweet side was nice though, and it was exactly what I needed after everything I'd been through.

When he finished drying me off and stepped away, I realized I didn't know some very basic information about the man I'd just declared my love for.

"I don't know your real name."

He paused toweling himself off to look at me with wide eyes. "Huh, guess it hasn't come up. My legal name is Kupono Beles. I wasn't keeping it from you on purpose or anything. It's just been such a long damn time since anyone has used it, I forget Trident isn't my only name most of the time."

I nodded, that made sense.

"My name was Grace Milani, Taz and Mum called me Gracie. You know, before the fire and I was put into witness protection. From then on, I was Jacie Lewis."

He nodded as he tossed the towel aside and took my hand again, leading me into the bedroom.

"Who picked your new name?"

I shrugged a shoulder again. "Not sure exactly. Because I was so young, they went with a name that was similar to my birth name, to make it easier for me to remember. And Lewis is my adoptive parents' last name. What about Trident? How'd that come about?"

I'd heard some crazy stories on how men had gotten their road names, and if the way Trident's cheeks just flushed red was any indication, his was going to be a good one.

Pulling back the sheets, he helped me in before he flipped on the bedside lamp then went to turn off the main light and check the door was locked. Once he was satisfied things were locked up, he came and joined me, lying on his side beside me.

"You sure you wanna know?"

I nodded, "Even more sure now that I see how nervous you are. C'mon, it can't be that bad."

Looking to the ceiling he blew out a breath and muttered something before focusing back on me.

"Not many know this story, and it needs to stay that way, we clear?"

I sat up, shifting so I faced him, more intrigued than ever. "Sure, it goes into my vault."

He huffed again. "Fine. When I was young and dumb, in my late teens. I used to chew gum all the time."

I nodded, "Trident brand, yeah?"

"That's the one. Well, one night, at a party at a classmate's house, me and a girl both had a little too much to drink and ended up in one of the bedrooms." He paused, giving his beard a tug. "Are you sure you need to know this shit?"

I was grinning, my heart feeling light at learning this secret part of my man that he'd shared with so few.

"Oh, you know I do. C'mon, T, just spit it out."

"Fine. I went down on her. But she wasn't shaved, and I still had my fucking gum in my mouth."

"Oh no. Are you telling me..." I covered my mouth with my hand.

He nodded, closing his eyes for a moment. "Yeah, my gum got stuck in her fucking pubic hair."

I snorted a laugh when I tried to hold it in, not wanting to make him feel worse than he already did.

"That's, um, sorry, T. But that's the funniest shit I've heard in a long time."

Chuckling, he grinned back. "Yeah, wasn't my finest moment."

"How'd you get the gum out? Please tell me you didn't give her a haircut."

"Peanut butter, not scissors. And before you ask, yes, I was a good boy and cleaned her up afterward. But she naturally told her friends about it, who told their friends and by the end of the school year everyone was calling me Trident. Yet another reason I had for wanting to go over to the mainland."

I was so giving him peanut butter and Trident gum on every one of our anniversaries. That was gold.

He was still looking extremely uncomfortable so I forced my humor aside and reached my arms out to him.

"With how orally fixated you are, I'm very grateful you've gotten better at going down on a woman since then. And with me being lasered, there's no worries of it happening again. Now, would you please come here and hold me. I'm so bloody tired, I feel like I could sleep for a week."

Within seconds, he was in the bed and had me pressed up against him, my back to his front, his arms around me. One hand cupping my pussy, the other a breast. He nuzzled into my neck, his beard tickling before he laid a kiss there.

"Night, *Ula'ula Mō'ī*. Sweet dreams."

"Hmmm, same to you, babe."

I was nearly asleep before I finished speaking.

Chapter 25

Trident

After waking a few times during the night to make love to my woman, we'd both slept in late the next morning. Would have stayed that way even longer if it wasn't for the bastard who'd started pounding on our damn door.

"C'mon, Trident! Get your woman and yourself outta bed already. You got visitors waiting on you."

That had me sitting up, jolting Jacie awake, and making her moan before she rolled over.

"What the fuck you mean I got visitors, Toa?"

His dark chuckle came through the closed door. "Oh, I ain't ruining their fun. You'll need to both come out here to see for yourselves. Just hurry up about it, *braddah*."

Muttering under my breath, I turned to roll Jacie over onto her back, covering her body with mine, kissing her awake. My cock was hard and throbbed against her soft pussy, and I would have given just about anything to have been able to slide in and fuck her again. But unfortunately I had to resist.

"C'mon, babe. We gotta get up and go see what the fuck Toa is on about with us having visitors."

With a hum, she wrapped her arms around my neck to pull me in for another kiss.

"It's probably my brother, with a bunch of Charons. Maybe my Dad, but I doubt Taz has told him much of anything yet. I certainly haven't."

Loved that she knew enough about how MCs worked that she'd known she couldn't bring her law enforcement father in if she wanted us to rescue her. And had trusted us over her fucking family to get the job done.

That had me freezing with a horrible thought: what if it was *my* family out there? I didn't doubt they could have heard by now that I was back on the island. I hadn't worried about trying to hide my face or anything when we'd gone through the airport because I'd figured they wouldn't have cared if word did get back to them. That and I'd been too preoccupied with getting Jacie back to give it much thought at all. But suddenly I was sure that's who was out there.

I pulled on what I'd worn yesterday while Jacie shrugged into a cute ankle length dress with big purple flowers on it that one of the local old ladies had gone out and bought for her yesterday. Looking down, she raised her palm to press over the tattoo, that the dress strap only partially covered. I went to her, pulling her in for a hug.

"No one will judge you for that war wound, babe. We can stick a bandage over it if you'd like. We can look into getting it removed or covered up once we get back home, yeah?"

She nodded. "A bandage would be good. I don't want to look at it, or have anyone else see it. And I'd already planned on getting it covered up. You know Eagle's old lady works and owns Silky Ink, right?"

I hadn't known that; but it wasn't like I'd spent a

heap of time studying all the Charon MC members. Jacie was the only one I'd ever looked into.

"I'm sure she'll take good care of you. Let me check the bathroom for that bandage, then we'll go see who's out there."

Thankfully, the cabinet was well stocked and I had no trouble finding a plaster big enough to fully cover her ink. Once I helped her put it on, and gave her another kiss, I took her hand and opened the door. As soon as we hit the hallway, I shook my head. How many damn people were here? It sounded like a lūʻau was going on in the main room.

Jacie cursed under her breath. "Did Toa invite the whole damn island? I have not had enough sleep for this kind of socializing."

I chuckled, nerves having me gripping her hand tight as we entered the large, crowded room that went silent on our arrival.

Nevaeh, Mirabelle and Sparrow all ran towards us, crashing into Jacie to hug her. They ended up pulling her away from me, her hand slipping from mine as they did. But I didn't fight it, just smiled as I watched her reconnect with her friends.

"Jacie! Omg!! I was about to go search for you so I could drag your butt outta bed. I am soo sorry! If I hadn't been teasing you, you wouldn't have snuck out by yourself and—"

"Nevaeh, enough. My uncle was set on getting me. He wouldn't have stopped until he grabbed me. If not yesterday, it would have been some other time. It's not your fault. If I hadn't been a mega bitch lashing out at everyone instead of processing my damn emotions like a grown arse adult, I wouldn't have been alone that morning either." Her eyes widened as she spun to face me. "What happened to Animal?"

Narrowing my gaze, I growled out the words. "He survived the surgery, but hasn't woken up yet so he's yet to answer for the part he played."

She detangled herself from the girls and I wrapped my arm around her once she was close enough to pull her in tight against me.

"He's not himself. He needs help, not punishment. Wait, you said surgery. What happened to him?"

"After he knocked you out, your uncle shot him in the shoulder. He's lucky Stone was following him and got to him in time to put pressure on the wound, or he would have bled out." Which might have been a mercy compared to what he was gonna get once he was out of the hospital.

She shook her head again. "Look, Animal will never be my favorite person, but you guessed right. He's addicted to some sort of pills. He was seriously strung out when he came into the cafe, and before he knocked me out, my uncle told him he needed to *finish the job*. Also, when my uncle asked him if he'd taken my phone, he lied. Told him he'd tossed it in the trash inside. It's because of Animal that I was able to message y'all to come get me."

Maverick spoke as he came up to us. "We'll take that into consideration when we decide the price he should pay, but you don't need to worry about him anymore, yeah? It's club business now."

She lowered her voice, clearly only wanting me and Maverick to hear her. "And the men yesterday?"

Maverick answered again. "Also club business, darlin'. All you need to know is that it's all cleaned up and no one who wasn't there, will ever know exactly what went down yesterday."

She rolled her eyes but didn't argue. I stiffened when I saw who was heading our way next.

Without taking my eyes off Jacie's brother, I whispered down to my woman who had buried her face in against my chest.

"Head's up, babe."

Taz looked rung out and like he hadn't slept in a week. Which he probably hadn't with his pregnant old lady not doing well, then his sister being fucking kidnapped.

"Hey there, sis. Can your brother get a hug?"

Before he'd finished speaking, Jacie had flung herself into his open arms with a gasp.

"Oh, Donny! I didn't think you'd be able to come. How's Flick? The baby?"

Folding my arms over my chest, I took in how carefully Taz held his sister. His eyes squeezed closed while he clutched her to him. It was clear he loved his sister dearly, and I prayed he would accept my claim over her, because I had no desire to fight the man.

"They're both doing fine. Flick's going nuts not being able to do anything, but she's feeling a lot better since we found out you're safe. Fuck, Gracie. You took ten years off my fucking life. You can't go doing this shit. I only just got you back."

I found it fucking adorable that they both reverted to using each other's birth names when they got emotional.

She chuckled, the sound watery as though she were crying, when she pulled back from her brother enough to look up into his face.

"Trust me, bro. I didn't exactly have a choice. Believe me, if I had, I wouldn't have done any of it."

He shook his head with a smirk at his sister's smart mouth before he hugged her tightly again. When he released her this time, he guided her back to me with a palm on her lower back.

He reached a hand out to me and I took it, accepting his handshake.

"Thank you, Trident. I know you went above and beyond, and we were fucking lucky you had contacts here that could help."

Emotion unexpectedly clogged my throat and I had to clear it before I could respond. "Your sister is my whole fucking world, Taz. I'd have done whatever it took to get her back."

He nodded. "So, I had a visitor before we flew out. Gave me something to pass on to you." He paused and looked me in the eye for a moment. "You serious about taking on my sister? She can be a handful, and such a brat."

"Oi!" Jacie lightly smacked at her brother's shoulder.

He raised an eyebrow her way. "You denying it?"

She blushed and shrugged a shoulder. "No, but it's rude to point it out!"

I laughed. "I know exactly who she is, and I love all of her, including the sass."

Taz grew serious again as Sparrow handed him a box.

"Well then, I pass this onto you with my blessing. But fucking hurt her, and I will come for you. You know I was one of the USMC's best snipers, right? You won't even know I'm onto you before you'll die. You hear me?"

"For fuck's sake, Taz! Really? Was that necessary."

He shrugged. "Seems fair to give the man a warning."

I huffed on a laugh. This whole family was fucking nuts.

"I'd heard your name thrown around some before I retired, so yeah, I know your skills. Good thing I never intend to hurt her."

I took the box from him, hoping it was what I wanted it to be. Maverick stepped up to hold it so I could open it up and sure enough, inside, wrapped in tissue paper was the cut I'd asked Viper to order in.

"Viper put it through church last night so it's all official and shit."

I grinned. "Fuck, he's a good man."

Maverick nodded. "The best. That's why he's pres."

Then I lifted the leather out and turned to my woman, who stood there, one arm wrapped around her middle, the other hand up near her mouth where she chewed on her thumbnail.

"Jacie, *Ula'ula Mõ'ī*, my red queen, will you accept my claim on you and wear my property patch?"

A shudder ran through her that had my breath catching. Would she really say no? Reject me in front of all these fucking people? She stepped forward and stroked her hand down the large patch on the back of the vest I was holding.

"In the past, I was pretty damn vocal about being against this whole concept. But after what happened, after experiencing what truly being owned by another person meant, I see that being an old lady; wearing a biker's property patch is something completely different."

She moved forward until she was pressed against my front. I had her cut in one hand, holding it to the side, as I wrapped the other arm around her waist.

"I'd never do a damn thing to hurt you, or clip your wings. I love you just the way you are, including that fiery temper of yours that can flare so damn fast it makes my head spin."

She grinned, her eyes sparkling with her humor. "Good thing that, because I ain't changing." Then she grew serious, cupping my bearded cheeks between her palms.

"I love you, *Kupono*. Just the way you are; possessive bastard and all."

Laughter bubbled up around us as we kissed, until someone tugged the leather from my hand. With a growl I looked up to see who'd be so stupid, but soon stopped when I saw Sparrow holding it out for Jacie to put on.

She gave me a shit-eating grin. "What? You were taking too long."

With a huff, I shook my head again. When that girl got claimed, she was gonna give her man so much trouble.

Maverick coughed to get my attention and I stiffened at the two people who were heading toward me.

"*Aloha* Makuahine; Makuakāne."

Jacie came back to my side, slipping her hand into mine and I gripped it tightly. I wasn't sure what else to say to my parents. They'd clearly aged in the decades since I'd last seen them, but they were achingly familiar. Fuck, I'd missed them so damn much. Tears stung my eyes as I waited to hear what they had to say.

"*Keiki*, did you read any of our letters?"

I shook my head at my father's question. "No. I'd still been too angry and hurt over what had happened, that and I needed to keep my focus on what I was doing on deployment."

He nodded, a grim look on his face. "I thought as much. I wish you had. You would have received our apologies a lot sooner and we wouldn't have lost so many years." He held my gaze with his own watery one. Damn, my dad was crying? "I'm sorry, keiki. I should have supported you. And I am very proud of all you've done, and the man you have become. I hope you can forgive us and allow us to get to know your woman and any grandkids you might give us in the future."

I had to clear my throat before I could respond. "Of course I forgive you. And I'm sorry for being such a damn hot head. I said things I shouldn't have too."

Before I could say more, Māmā pounced on me, sobbing and wrapping her arms around me. Releasing Jacie, I embraced my mother, rubbing her back as she wet my shoulder with her tears.

Damn, who would have thought this was how this trip was going to end? I got my family back, claimed and patched the perfect woman as my own, and reconnected with Toa.

The future was looking pretty damn bright all of the sudden.

Want to know about new relcases, events and other news? Get a free ebook?
Sign up for my author newsletter at the following link:
https://newsletter.khloewren.com/trident_signup

Thank you so much for reading Trident. I hope you enjoyed reading Trident and Jacie's story as much as I did writing it and would love it if you could leave a review. If you'd like to know what happens when Taz first discovers his sister is alive, keep reading for a snippet from Taz's Guards, Book 14 in the Charon MC

As I headed from the vehicle toward the building with my Beretta in my palm, the sound of several Harleys filled the air. My club brothers coming to have my back. Would Mac be with them? Would Scout? I wasn't sure how to wrap my mind around them keeping such big secrets about my past from me, but it wasn't something I was gonna sort out at the moment. Now, it was time to make sure my old lady and daughter were safe.

And work out who the fuck else was in that house.

With my weapon raised and ready to fire, I began to climb onto what was left of the front porch. The door swung open and when Flick appeared in the doorway clutching Lolly to her, I shifted my aim to the space beside Flick's head, on the opposite side from Lolly. I didn't want to have to risk a shot so close to either of my girls, but if a threat stood behind them, I could take care of it if necessary.

Check out the following link for ebook links to keep reading:
reading:
https://books2read.com/TazsGuards

Acknowledgments

As always, my family is amazing and supports me through writing each of my books. This one was no exception. Well, unless you count them having to do more than usual as an exception. Steve took on a lot of the chores around the house in the last month or so of my writing Trident, as I was running out of time and was desperately trying to get it finished in time for MMM25. Elodie thankfully loves to cook, and loves to read, so she often came home to cook meals for us or just to sit beside me to make sure I didn't get distracted. She also chose the drinks the characters drunk in this book, as she's currently studying for a Diploma in Hospitality and loved learning how to make/mix various drinks.

I found myself needing to find a new editor early on in this project and because I also needed it done in a very short time frame, in the end used two ladies. I can't thank Cass and Andrea enough for their late nights and hard work on this project. An extra shoutout to Andrea whose knowledge of Hawaiian and MC culture helped immensely.

So much research went into this project. Firstly, a thanks to Jo Carol and the BLC team who put on the annual writers retreat in Kaua'i, without which, I wouldn't have thought to include the island into a story. Jo Carol's daughters, Brandy & Brit: Thank you for not only sharing the hilarious story about the boy with the gum, but for letting me borrow it for Trident's character. Jose, not only are you the perfect cover model for

Trident in looks, but it turns out in lifestyle too! Thank you for all your Hawaiian and MC help, and all the other support you and your lovely wife, Andrea, have given me.

My fellow Red Queen, Dorothy F. Shaw, how to find the words to express my extreme gratitude? Without our daily sprints this book definitely wouldn't have gotten written. You've picked me up when I've fallen, kicked my arse when required, helped brainstorm things when I got stuck, and offered me all the information I needed to write in Animal's addiction issues (spoiler alert: he will be redeemed in a later book!)

CT Creations, thank you for the spectacular cover and for fitting in a rush job on the print wrap for me.

Lastly, to you who's reading this. Without my readers, I wouldn't be able to do this job that I absolutely love doing. So thank you for your loyalty and patience with me. It's been a rough couple of years with both my physical and mental health, which has meant I've not published much at all. In fact, this book is the first new story I've written since my AuDHD diagnosis and starting meds. I hope you enjoy reading Trident as much as I enjoyed writing it.

xo

Khloe Wren

About the Author

USA Today bestselling author, Khloe Wren, lives in rural South Australia with her husband, two daughters and an ever-changing list of animals! She started writing in 2012 and has published over 50 romantic suspense books since then. She writes both paranormal and contemporary stories, including her best-selling series The Charon MC. Khloe loves to lean into her AuDHD, following her muse down research rabbit holes to bring diverse characters and storylines to life.

Khloe loves to hear from readers, so please check out the links below to keep in touch:

Website:
http://www.khloewren.com
FaceBook:
http://www.facebook.com/authorkhloewren
Instagram:
https://www.instagram.com/khloewren/
Street Team:
https://www.facebook.com/groups/85638334446051 4/
Newsletter:
https://newsletter.khloewren.com/sign_up